My family and other idiots

Kay Carlton

Email: kaycarltonauthor@gmail.com

Dedication

For all the friends and family that made 2020 easier, especially my 2 human lockdown buddies, and our little fur buddy. I Love you all

So it's now 2020 - I'm in year 10 and Boris is in charge of the country.

SERIOUSLY … BORIS !??!!!??

My stepdad Neville thinks Boris is an idiot. Mind you ….. he's a fine one to talk.

Apparently Boris won the election because he said he'd 'Get Brexit Done' and everyone hates Jeremy Corbyn. I don't know why. He's a bit scruffy and he looks a bit like a geography teacher, but I'm not sure why that means he can't be a Prime Minister. Boris isn't exactly tidy looking - his hair is ridiculous ….

Anyway …. loads of things happened last year, but Brexit wasn't one of them - even though everyone went ON and ON about it.

Stuff that DID happen :

* A song about sausage rolls was the Christmas No.1 for the 2nd year in a row
* Some scientists managed to teach rats to drive little cars
* An egg was the most liked photo on instagram - it beat Kylie Jenner !
* Caitlyn Jenner was on 'I'm a Celebrity'
* There was a viral challenge where you had to kick the cap off of a bottle (Neville kept trying, which was very funny and SO embarrassing)
* Game of Thrones finished, after like a MILLION years (Neville spent weeks moaning about the ending)
* There was soooooo much drama at school it was just UNBELIEVABLE
* We had to pick our GCSE subjects (so boring)

Oh … and I actually had a REAL boyfriend for a while.

If you don't know anything about my family, here's a really quick explanation. There's me Ruby - I'll be 16 this year. There's my Mum Jaz (real name Janice) who is into loads of spiritual, weird, hippy nonsense. She buys lots of self-help books and crystals and wears strange floaty clothes. She is a TOTAL embarrassment. Neville is my stepdad. He's pretty embarrassing as well, mostly because of the TERRIBLE band that he's in, they actually play in places around town! CRINGING. He is mostly OK, but he likes to complain A LOT, he complains about … well … everything really. I've got 2 really little cousins Felix and Coco, they belong to Auntie Sophie and Uncle Marc. My oldest cousin is Ella, she's at Uni, she's Uncle Dave and Auntie Sally's daughter. There's Auntie Ellie - we don't see her very often as she has a really important job and is always busy going to important meetings around the world. Then there's Uncle John - he lives in America. He had Jaime with my Auntie Mindy and they got divorced and he had Chad and Brad (who are twins) with Emmy-Lou . There's Grandma and Grandpa - who are like .. typical grandparents. Then there's Em, Alice and Charlotte - who are my BEST friends.

Mum has a LOT of close girlfriends - the main ones are Lizzy, Bridget, Jane, Helen, Rachel, Margaret, Suzie, Cath, Jo and The Turbot (that's not her real name). The main thing they ALL have in common is drinking lots and behaving like stupid children. I'm more mature than they are.

She has a new friend Martha Appleby .. she REALLY didn't like her before ..The Applebys were like this ridiculously PERFECT family that used to annoy her (and Neville) .. but that changed. Mum always says "never judge a book by it's cover, Ruby you can be very, very wrong."

Then there are few people that Mum and Neville just moan about .. there's Ollie (he used to be Neville's boss, but now he owns this trendy vegan cafe) - he's very young and very successful. I think he's nice. I think Neville's just jealous. There's Jasmine - her daughter Chloe is at my school. Now I know for a fact that Mum is DEFINITELY jealous of her. She has this amazingly successful travel/fashion/wellness blog. Finally there's Debbie - she's nice enough, but she's one of those people that spills her WHOLE life on social media - like every SINGLE day - which might be alright if her life was exciting, but unfortunately most of her life revolves around one of her many, many kids being ill. Neville says they must have had every disease known to man … even ones that haven't been discovered yet.

Oh and I forgot - there's also Izzy, my EX friend. Jake, my EX boyfriend. And last of all… the idiot dog.

So … where was I? Oh yeah. It's New Year's Day - 1st January 2020 - it's a NEW YEAR and a NEW DECADE and EVERYONE is going on about how amazing it's going to be.

After the total disaster of Chemical Banana performing last new year's eve (Chemical Banana are Neville's terrible band), they decided to give it a miss this year and just get drunk in the pub. He is still not up, but there is what looks like the remains of a disgusting kebab in the kitchen. The idiot dog obviously knows there is some kind of meat left lying about (IF you can call that grey looking stuff meat) and has been jumping vertically in the air next to the worktop for the last hour. Neville finally got up, put the kettle on, looked at the dog, and said, "What's with the Maasai Warrior impression."

I have no idea what he is talking about - he's probably still drunk.

New year's eve was really fun for me this year - mostly because I went to Em's house to get away from Mum.

Mum is STILL on her whole 'spiritual journey' thing … Honestly !! She gets more and more weird. She wanted to stay in alone and have an 'end of year self-love ceremony' whatever THAT is. She said she was going to write out all the toxic things she's let go of this year on special paper that's infused with energy and burn them in a cleansing ritual. I had no intention of being around for that. Neville called it 'utter b*llocks' and stomped to the pub.

Mum and Neville have decided they are doing 'Dry January' again - I don't know why they bother. It was a total disaster last year. Neville messed up by going to the pub on the FIRST DAY. He is claiming that January 1st doesn't count. He said, "An old Irish friend of mine used to give up alcohol every year for Lent, but he always said he had a special dispensation from The Pope to get wasted on St Patrick's Day, this is a bit similar."

Honestly!! I'm sure The Pope has more important things to be doing and of course it COUNTS - it's literally the first day of January!

So yeah .. it's a new year, but I seriously can't get that excited. My phone screen has gone weird and the phone KEEPS switching itself off .. it's a total disaster. Neville says he won't get me a new one because it's not due to be upgraded for 3 months. 3 MONTHS !!!! How does he expect me to cope for 3 months with a crap phone?????????

He just says stuff like, "Come and talk to me when you've got an ACTUAL problem Ruby. Talk about bloody spoilt !!! All I got when I was your age was a hand-me-down coat and a clip round the ear."

OMG he's ANNOYING - why doesn't he get it !!!!!! How can he say that I'm spoilt, I mean SERIOUSLY???? It's only an iPhone 7 .. it's SOOOOOOO embarrassing, no-one has a phone that old apart from me.

It's an absolute NIGHTMARE …. I literally have to hide it at school and just use my Apple Watch.

****

So …. the last time I was really writing lots of stuff in my journal was when me and Jake JUST kind of started getting together - which was the end of 2018.

2019 kind of flew by really fast ….. TBH I didn't write that much at all - there are loads of empty pages and big gaps everywhere.

It started out OK, but then I got distracted with TikTok and spent most of my time on there …. AND I got distracted with Jake of course … and a bunch of other dramas … but I'm going to try to write more this year .. if I have the time .. but who knows me and the girls have TONS of plans so I'll probably be out ALL the time and just too busy to do it.

But .. just so you can catch up, this is a quick summary of some of the stuff I remember happened last year and some stuff that I did actually write down at the time:

January 2019

1st January

Today is New Year's Day 2019 - Neville's been sulking all day - his band stupidly decided to do a gig for New Year and were pretty much laughed out of the pub. They were SO BAD that apparently Mum and her friends left after about 10 minutes and went to another pub. He's been ranting about loyalty for the last hour and stuffing bacon sandwiches into his face like someone that's been starved for weeks.

Mum is drinking A LOT of tea and looks VERY rough. There is still a bit of mascara smudged under her eyes. No doubt she got all emotional about New Year, crying and telling all her friends how much she loves them.

Thank goodness I was at Grandma's for the night. The most embarrassing thing that went on there was Grandpa insisting we did the Hokey Cokey at midnight.

I don't know what that was all about.

Grandma kept telling him that you are supposed to sing Old Lan Sign (or something like that?) But we did the Hokey Cokey in the middle of the lounge anyway. The London fireworks were pretty cool on TV, but then they put someone called Jools Holland on, which was even less exciting than the Hokey Cokey, so I went to bed.

Mum is busy with her 'intentions' list for 2019. She doesn't believe in New Year's Resolutions. She said these are entirely "fuelled by the media and the diet industry and designed to make people feel bad about themselves." She is working out 'feelings goals' for the year based on how she wants to feel and not "arbitrary numbers on a set of scales." She said, "People set themselves up for failure choosing things they think they SHOULD be doing, rather than things they feel passionate about."

Neville said, "Well I feel quite passionate about getting rid of this hangover. I'm off to the pub for a pint."

Mum said, "You should write out some intentions Ruby. It's inspiring. I am reviewing all the successes and achievements of 2018 and setting new intentions for the coming year. I need a word of the year .... last year my word was GROWTH."

SERIOUSLY????

If anyone had bothered to ask me, I could have told them the word of 2018 was definitely SHED!!!!!! Which, by the way, has STILL not been bought even though they argued about it for like a WHOLE year. Honestly HOW does anyone spend that much time talking about something SO DULL? But just before Christmas, Mum made Neville promise (under threat of being divorced immediately), that he will buy one as soon as we've cleared the costs from Christmas.

January 4th

So Mum and Neville are doing 'Dry January' and 'Veganuary.' We had some disgusting meals for like the first 3 days and then they gave up!! A typical example was her spending hours cooking dinner, just when I was hoping for some of the gammon leftovers from new year, but we had some vegan thing with loads of chickpeas instead. It was disgusting, I had two spoonfuls and got myself some gammon anyway. Neville said, "It's very nice Jaz, and Brexit has ruined gammon for me anyway."

Seriously - why do they bring Brexit into everything.

Neville also said, "The chances of your mother staying off both wine and cheese for a whole month are about as likely as Theresa May getting her Brexit deal approved by Parliament."

Ever since the Sausage Roll song got to number 1, Neville's been obsessed with Lad Baby - he's been watching all the YouTube videos (I notice HIM watching "shit on YouTube" is OK .. another example of what hypocrites the two of them are). I told him to watch the ones where they decorate each other's cars - it's so funny. She puts all pictures of her face and love hearts all over his car and he gets her back by putting a big picture of himself eating a sausage roll on her car.

Speaking of sausage rolls - Neville spent most of January in a really bad mood because Greggs brought out a Vegan Sausage Roll for Veganuary. There was loads of moaning about it on Twitter and Facebook. People seem to be really angry about it. Goodness knows why. Apart from Greggs - they are really happy, and must be "laughing all the way to the bank" as Grandma says. I always picture a bunch of people walking in a line towards the bank laughing in a demented way - that makes me smile actually. Anyway, apparently the vegan sausage rolls ended up "flying off the shelves" and Greggs were struggling to keep up with the demand. Piers Morgan (who used to be on Britain's Got Talent) ranted about it quite a lot. Neville said, "It's a sad day when I agree with something that massive tw*t Piers Morgan has to say."

I really don't see what the problem is - loads of people are vegan, if Greggs want to make a sausage roll for them what's wrong with that??

They aren't doing anyone any harm - so stupid. I wouldn't be surprised if it's got something to do with Brexit - everything else has!

January 18th

It's the 18th day of Dry January and they gave up ages ago - Neville keeps saying they are now doing "Damp January". After just 2 days they were moaning it was hard work and Neville had already messed up once. Mum said, "It's a good opportunity for you to prove to Ollie that you can manage without using beer as an emotional crutch."

(As usual I don't understand half of what she goes on about ... crutches are for broken legs ... they don't have emotions...)

Anyway - the comment really annoyed him (Ollie's his boss and he's really jealous of him because he's successful and very young!). Neville said, "I have absolutely NOTHING to prove to that sanctimonious little git Jaz." Then he said, "mind you, he's doing my performance review tomorrow. Maybe I will take him one of those Greggs vegan sausage rolls to butter him up."

Then he started laughing and saying, "See what I did there? Aye? Butter him up? Vegans don't eat butter ! Funny hey?"

Honestly! He should look up the word funny on Wikipedia!

I was really nervous about going back to school (I wrote LOADS about that .. which is REALLY BORING looking back on it). It was mainly because I was nervous about bumping into Jake Lakson. We'd started linking in the holidays so I thought it might be weird when I actually saw him.

February 2019:

There was loads of arguing in the family WhatsApp this month about some terrorist girl that wanted to come back to England. She ran off to Syria to join ISIS when she was 15, and then wanted to come back to the UK, because she was pregnant.

This is what I wrote …

The family's arguing about some ISIS terrorist. Grandpa keeps saying, "It's all well and good deciding you've changed your mind and want to come back to the UK, but she joined a terrorist group, she should be bloody banned. All this crap about human rights, a bloody nonsense if you ask me ... she ran off to join a group of people that want us all dead."

Auntie Sophie said, "I think you need to stop reading The Telegraph Dad - it makes you very angry." Grandma said, "Some horrible looking woman called Katie Hopkins has released a video about it on Facebook and said she doesn't get to call England home anymore."

Hang on a minute ... since when is Grandma on Facebook?

Mum said, "Ignore Katie Hopkins Mum, she is a nasty, poisonous human being you don't want to listen to anything that woman has to say."

Grandpa said, "Well even the Home Secretary is saying this girl should be kept out."

Then Auntie Ellie joined in and said, "Let's not lose sight of the fact she was a radicalised minor, a victim of fundamentalist grooming."

So Mum said, "Rubbish Ellie, she may have been a minor, but she knew exactly what she was doing, now you know normally I am all about forgiveness and moving on ... but she doesn't even seem sorry.. ."

Ella joined in and said, "I dunno why everyone's going on about this girl ... and anyway .... what's ISIS? My friend's dog is called that I think."

Then a message popped up saying, "Jack Brady has left the group." Grandpa is getting less and less patient these days, especially with Ella.

Neville and Mum were STILL talking about this girl wanting to come back to the UK at dinner time. Neville said, "She's not showing remorse, she doesn't regret going there, she just wants her kid to be safe, which I get, but if she was showing the tiniest bit of guilt it might be a different kettle of fish."

That's another weird expression .... Why would you put fish in a kettle?? I asked Grandma and it turns out a "fish kettle" is completely different to a kettle you use to make tea. Maybe I should have made Mum and Neville a cup of tea to calm them down? That always works on the T.V. on the soaps and stuff.

*They'd finally stopped banging on about ISIS and decided to watch something on Netflix, when I went to say goodnight. They were just settling down on the sofa, flicking through the channels and Neville said, "I don't know Jaz, we are only a few weeks into 2019 and so far I've agreed with both Katie Hopkins and Piers Morgan about something .... the world's a right f***ing mess!"*

****

Also Auntie Ellie's VERY LATE Christmas presents arrived in February. She'd apparently been working crazy hours preparing important economic stuff for another one of her big meeting things. Some world economic forum or whatever with loads of important people. So she didn't have time to visit us at Christmas or send presents. She had time to go skiing apparently, but she said that's because it's vital she "retain her form on the slopes." Whatever.

I wasn't happy about the gift according to my journal ..

I complained to Mum, because my present was a bunch of cards from Oxfam that said "I got you Education for a Child" on the front. Mum said, "Education changes everything for children in the Third World Ruby, it gives them opportunities to get better jobs or start businesses and work their way out of poverty. It's a really generous gift, it's helping 10 different children have a better future."

Neville said, "Count yourself lucky Ruby - I got a pile of poo."

I must have looked really confused because Mum said, "Ignore him Ruby, it's a special programme providing pigs and a biodigester thing to a village, and it turns the pig poo into gas so people can cook with it. It's REALLY clever ! And it means women don't have to walk miles every day to get firewood. It gives them time and freedom to do other things. Honestly Neville, even you'd have to agree that's really clever."

But he just said, "Well I didn't ACTUALLY read it Jaz, it says, "I got you a pile of poo," and there was a picture of a load of turds on the front. That's not a gift."

March 2019

Jake officially became my boyfriend. It was so exciting. But I didn't tell Mum because she would TOTALLY embarrass me.

Also it was Book week in March. I wrote about that .. it's always cute.

7th March

It's dress up day for World Book Week. I had an INSET day too so I got to see loads of the little kids walking to school in their outfits .. it was the cutest !!

I used to love doing Book Week. I remember going as Verucca Salt from Charlie and the Chocolate Factory, one of the 101 Dalmatians and Fern from Charlotte's Web. I had wellie boots on and a cuddly pig under my arm. A boy in my class just went as The Boy in the Dress every single year. Grandpa always used to moan about kids going dressed as Disney characters and people from films, and not dressing up as characters from real books. I remember he took me into school one year when I was the mouse from The Gruffalo and he kept saying stuff really loudly like, "Look at that boy, he's dressed as Buzz Lightyear - that's not a book, it's a bloody Pixar film. It's called World Book Day for a reason, it's a bloody nonsense."

I saw a couple of Paddingtons; a Stickman; and a really clever Captain Underpants outfit. There were two really tiny kids, who looked like twins, they were Little Miss Sunshine and Mr Happy - they were running along the road looking sooooo excited. Ridiculously cute. There were tons of Harry Potters; loads of Elsas (even though Frozen is a film not a book - Grandpa wouldn't like that); a Mary Poppins and at least 2 Peter Rabbits.

The Applebys had obviously been working on their costumes for EVER. We saw LOADS of photos of them posted all over Facebook. Jennifer (Mum's friend that knows them really well) told Mum that Archie Appleby originally wanted to go as Harry Potter, but Mrs Appleby wouldn't let him, she said "every man and his dog" would be Harry Potter and it wasn't inventive enough. Alice Appleby went as the White Witch from the Narnia books. She had the most incredible white fur outfit, amazing make up with what looked like icy diamonds on her face and this UNBELIEVABLE ice crown that looked like real icicles. I have literally NO IDEA how Mrs Appleby made it! Mum said, "She actually looks even better than Tilda Swinton did in the film." Archie was the BFG. She made him massive ears, a waistcoat and a cape. He had a huge dreamcatcher net and a dream blower horn. The horn looked like a really, really big sink plunger sprayed gold. Mum said it probably was a sink plunger, because Mrs Appleby is very creative and could make anything look brilliant.

Then Mum said, "I've finally decided that my word for 2019 is going to be CREATIVITY. I want to explore my creative soul this year. I sat with the word JOY for a long time, but something wasn't quite right at a soul level. I think I might take up watercolour painting or pottery. I could create an "artistic corner" in my meditation shed."

*Neville said, "Alright, Janice, alright. You win, I will sort the shed out and you can do what the f**k you want with it. But if your version of being creative is making decorative sink plungers, you can piss right off."*

Then he said, "I forgot to tell you, I actually walked past the Applebys when I was out with the dog this morning. Alice was having a proper screaming meltdown, said her ice crown was hurting her head and Archie just kept shouting, "I hate this stupid outfit, I don't want to wear these big stupid ears all day." I heard Terence Appleby swear under his breath and say, "FFS Martha, why couldn't you just let the little shit go as Harry Potter ??

Mum said Debbie's youngest missed out on dressing up for Book Week because she'd been up all night being sick. Debbie was really upset especially because she'd got a Hermoine Granger outfit delivered just in time by Amazon Prime. There were 127 "OMG so sorry Hun, hope she feels better," responses on Facebook.

Easter Holidays

OMG - so in the Easter Break we went on this amazing holiday to Bali - I missed a couple of days at the end of term because it was a really long way to travel. It was for Mum & Neville's 10 wedding anniversary (goodness knows how they've put up with one another for 10 years - but that's another story). Anyway she said there were loads of bits of the country she hadn't seen, because when she went there on this retreat a few years ago, they just stayed in their amazing villa and didn't travel around.

So we went for 2 and a bit weeks and stayed in all these cool Airbnb places. Everyone was called Kadek.. or Wayan. I basically did loads of vlogging & instagramming and didn't write anything down AT ALL. Mainly because everywhere was really gorgeous.... like the beach clubs and the infinity pools, and these cool cafes, that were decorated just so you could take some great shots for insta - so I just took TONS of pictures. The flight was really long, but it was pretty cool. Also I saw a sea turtle when we went snorkelling.

I got a really good tan for once and my instafeed looked AMAZING. Chloe was ACTUALLY jealous of me for once (that's never happened !!) because Jasmine goes to loads of exotic places, but she NEVER EVER takes Chloe. She says it's because it's 'work' - but most of it looks like one big holiday to me. She also says it's important to have time alone to relax, restore and rejuvenate her body and her mind. Neville said he thought it was totally ridiculous that someone that "writes a bit of b*llocks on the internet a couple of times a week" needed to rejuvenate. He said, "it's not like it's actual WORK.. she'd know about it if she had to do a real job."

Sometimes he sounds exactly like Grandpa.

April 2019

Notre Dame Cathedral nearly burnt down! Well, a big chunk of it did, some of it is still there. Mum was really upset. She loves Paris.

We went there for a weekend with my cousin Jaime a couple of years ago .. Mum was banging on about museums all the time and made us get this boat thing around the Seine instead of getting on the Metro, so we could "really appreciate the beauty of Paris." She kept talking about places I'd never heard of (apart from the Eiffel Tower) and calling it the City of Light. She's been to Paris loads of times, but the rest of us had never been and she thought we'd be really excited about it.

I quite liked some of it. I liked sitting at the little cafes on the street, all in a row, people watching. And I did actually like Notre Dame, but we had to get up really really EARLY to catch the Eurostar so we were really tired the day we went on the boat. Me and Neville both fell asleep on the way round and Jaime just spent the whole time on Snapchat to her American mates and didn't look at the views once. Mum tried to get Jaime to put her phone away, but she just kept saying, "they are just waking up in the US, are you gonna stop me speaking to my friends??"

Mum ended going off for a walk on her own because she was in such a bad mood about it. It was only a stupid boat ride - I don't know why she was so bothered.

OMG - I nearly forgot the most important thing that happened ALL YEAR (well apart from me & Jake going out). Neville finally bought the shed !!!! He had it delivered and even paid extra for some men to actually put the shed up. Good job - if he'd have done it I wouldn't be surprised if it had fallen straight down.

Mum started decorating it immediately - she'd collected all these draped bits of sparkly cloth and weird symbols. She made Neville run power cables from the house so she could have fairy lights and play relaxing music. Well ..... she didn't ACTUALLY make Neville do it ... that might have led to someone getting electrocuted ... Pete the electrician from round the corner came over and did it.

May 2019

A new girl has started in our class. She is called Emma and her family just moved back here after spending 6 years in New Zealand. She has a really strong accent and it sounds like "pin" when she says "pen" and "iggs" when she says "eggs." It's a really nice accent. She is really lovely and is very shy. She's been sitting with me, Em, Izzy, Alice and Charlotte most days. Izzy said she's fine being friends with her, because she's really ordinary looking and there isn't much to be jealous about. That's so mean - she is really superficial. I asked her if that meant she thinks all of us are "ordinary" and "not pretty enough to be jealous of," but she got all embarrassed and said, "I didn't mean it like that. It's just that Emma's hair's a really boring colour and she wears glasses." Then she tried to say that we are all gorgeous, and Emma really suits her glasses, but it was a bit late. We all walked out and left her sitting on her own in the canteen.

Mum said, "If Izzy goes through life making decisions purely based on how attractive people are, she will never have any meaningful relationships. People are just too hung up on looks these days - especially all these celebrity Instagram accounts - it sets SUCH a bad example, especially for young girls. It's not about what's on the outside that matters, it's what's on the inside."

Neville said, "Yes that's absolutely right Ruby, if I was bothered about people looking perfect, I wouldn't be with your mother now would I?"

Mum said, "Well thank you very much." Then she burst into tears and ran off upstairs.

He said, "Oh shit. Here we go, I didn't mean it like that Ruby, I was only having a laugh. I agree with her about the fact that it's what's on the inside that counts and all that stuff."

I told him, "Well you've done it now! I went to check on Mum, but she must have gone in the bath. She usually takes her phone so I texted her some love hearts and a little message saying "Neville is a complete idiot." That should cheer her up.

Mum literally hasn't spoken to Neville for 2 days. She walks out of a room as soon as he walks into it and hasn't made ANY dinner for him for the last two nights or tonight. He's existing entirely on things with oven chips. Sausage and chips, egg and chips, beans and chips. He's got no idea about cooking. To make it worse Mum has made some really nice meals for me and her.

He brought her a big box of Maltesers on Tuesday. She said to me, "kindly tell Neville that I no longer eat refined sugar" (She DOES .. but I told him anyway) then she went off to shut herself in the shed to listen to weird music in her 'sacred corner.' I pinched the box of Maltesers and hid them in my room.

Yesterday he brought her some special salted caramel ice-cream and a cute card saying 'To me you are perfect.' She tore that up in front of him, then walked off saying, "kindly tell Neville that I no longer eat dairy products."

Then today, he came in from work with a MASSIVE bunch of flowers - like really nice ones from M&S - not crappy ones from a garage. She just brushed past him without a word and went for a long bath.

I put the flowers in a vase - they looked really pretty in the kitchen. I told Neville she'd probably enjoy looking at them when he wasn't around.

He said, "I'm running out of ideas Ruby. I hate it when your mother is upset. What can I do to say sorry?"

I told him maybe he should take her out for a nice meal and spoil her a bit on Friday night. But he said Chemical Banana had a gig which was much more important. So much for hating it when she's upset !

Neville was looking pretty miserable actually and Mum's been a right pain so I decided to take matters into my own hands. I made him book a table at the nice Italian place and sent him out to buy her a voucher for a special facial treatment that makes you look younger.

When Mum got back from yoga I told her that there is enough pressure on me as a teenager as it is, and the two of them not speaking is making me more stressed, and she wouldn't want to be responsible for causing me issues with anxiety. I told her Neville was taking her out for dinner and that there was a gift on the kitchen worktop and she needed to start speaking to him again.

That seemed to do the trick. I heard her say, "Neville, for god's sake don't stand around looking gormless, make yourself useful, unpack the dishwasher or something." Well I suppose that counts as them speaking again.

I found the film of Gangster Granny on Netflix, dug out the box of Maltesers I'd hidden and ate the whole lot while they were out for dinner.

Also in May, Meghan and Harry had a baby boy called Archie and Theresa May resigned. It was pretty embarrassing really … she rattled on about how much she loved our country and that it had been an honour. Then cried outside Downing Street. Honestly! She looks absolutely terrible .. you think she'd be glad not to be the Prime Minister anymore……

June 2019

16th June

We've started calling Emma "Kiwi Em" now so we don't mix her up with Em Em. Turns out she fancies Dan and he fancies her. He's been to New Zealand with his family - they've been talking about it on Snapchat and then they started linking. Izzy is SOOOOOO jealous about it. Which is ridiculous since she hasn't even talked to Dan since term started. She keeps saying really bitchy things about Kiwi Em and going "only joking" straight after.

Auntie Sophie and Uncle Marc came to visit this weekend. They are trying to potty train Felix. He keeps taking his nappies off and pooing in anything that looks a bit like a potty. He pooed in one of Grandma's flower pots last week. He also ripped his nappy off one day and Auntie Sophie literally had to catch this big poo before it landed on her really nice rug.

On Saturday morning he ran in from the garden holding a poo in his hand and gave it to Auntie Sophie. Auntie Sophie said, "Felix, did you do a poo? Is this your poo? Tell Mummy. DID YOU do this poo?" but he just laughed at her and ran off. Auntie Sophie said that he sometimes takes the poos out of his nappy instead of taking the nappy off, but Neville said he thought that one belonged to the dog.

Everyone spent ages swopping poo stories - so embarrassing - Mum even told a couple of stories from when I was tiny. NOT FUNNY.

20th June

Izzy is REALLY getting on my nerves. Just because she was annoyed about Dan and Kiwi Em, she's been deliberately trying to flirt with Jake - which is really mean of her and NOT how a friend should carry on.

There wasn't really anything else written for June. I think it's because I was so upset with Izzy, I just spent more time chatting with Em on FaceTime and doing loads of TikToking to take my mind off having to deal with Izzy. Mum always just says stuff like, "ignore her Ruby," and "hang out with other people," and "sometimes you need to remove toxic people from your life", but that's pretty hard to do when we all sit together at school.

July 2019

The term ended really badly - I'm not speaking to Izzy anymore. She totally stole Jake from me. She was flirting with him all the time - BEHIND MY BACK - and it turned out they were talking on FaceTime and she was constantly sending him photos and videos of her posing and pouting in really slaggy outfits.

It was a good job the summer holidays started - because it meant I didn't have to see them together. I saw them across the field by the football pitches one day, but went the other way before they saw me. She tried to send me a few messages saying that she misses me and she loves me and a load of other rubbish. I totally ghosted her. I don't even care. I have plenty of MUCH better friends.

Kiwi Em's Mum has joined Mum's gang - Mum says she's really fun and "likes a drink" - well that's handy since all her and her mates do is drink !

Her name is Debbie, but she still has quite a strong accent so it sounds like "Dibbie" - so everyone calls her Dibbie so they don't confuse her with the other Debbie. Mind you Neville started calling the other Debbie "Typhoid Debbie" even before there was someone else with the same name. He has names for everyone - he has two old school mates called Big John and Shat-himself-John. I don't know why he's a BIG John when there isn't a LITTLE John and I REALLY don't want to know about the other one! He's also good mates with Polio Steve; Dick the Prick (actually called Richard); Council House Dave; Pervy Dave and Dave the Leper . He's no longer friends with someone who he calls either "that arrogant twat" and "He who shall not be named" (like in Harry Potter).

We've literally only got Em and Kiwi Em and James 1 & 2. Boring really.

Also they announced that Boris Johnson was taking over from Theresa May. Neville said he can't POSSIBLY do a worse job as Prime Minister.

August 2019

Summer was boring - we went to Wales for a few days. Mum said the trip to Bali had cost a fortune so we wouldn't be going away for ages. Everyone else was on holiday (like always) so it was pretty dull, but I made the best of it and actually it went by pretty quick. The weather was OK, so I got a bit of a tan.

It was nice in Wales - we stayed in a really sweet Airbnb. Em came as there were two beds in my room and we went to Zip World which was cool. Me and Em did some shopping and wandered about on our own - there was a little garden to sunbathe and we were near a lovely harbour. Mum and Neville did what they wanted and we did what we wanted so it was pretty good. While we were there Izzy did something really really nasty. Me and her set up a TikTok channel together in June before we stopped talking to one another. She hardly posted anything on it (just the odd pouting picture and some very BAD singing) but I posted loads of stuff that people really liked. Then, in Wales, I did this whole series of videos that got like a MILLION views and like 300k followers.

These were my journal entries. Urghh - STILL makes me angry:

12th August

OMG I can't believe it .. there are sooo many people liking the videos and asking me to do a follow up story .. it's amazing. Me and Em keep checking the numbers, it's so cool. The account just reached 200k followers ... the views are just going up and up too ... amazing !!

13th August

OMG - Izzy has done something sooo totally bitchy - it's unbelievable. The Jake thing was bad enough but this is EVEN worse !! The account had even more followers today and she just sent a message saying that because the account has her email address attached to it, it's HER account so she's taking my name off it and using it to promote her 'modelling career.'

It's soooo unfair - I'm sooooo glad Em is on holiday with us too because no one would believe she's done this. Em sent her a bunch of really nasty messages saying the only reason the account is successful is MY videos and not HER slaggy photos !! She can't just TAKE the account - it's all my followers ...!! It's like 700k NOW !!

Mum said to talk to her about it without being angry or nasty and just ask that she change the email address so I keep the account because I've done all the work. I tried that, but she refused. She's such a sneaky skank !!

Mum said, "why doesn't she just start a new account for her modelling, I don't get it ?" ARHghghhghhhh - I keep telling her she won't because she wants to steal my fans. I HATE HER SOOOOOOOOO MUCH.

She doesn't even have a 'modelling career' she just gets dressed in clothes that are too tight and puts waaaaay too much makeup on and pouts. THAT'S IT ! She's never even had a proper photo shoot. The M's just take pictures of each other posing all the time - not even good pictures. It's embarrassing...

Neville saw one and said, "Blimey - most of her isn't even IN that dress... barely covers her arse."

Grandma didn't understand why I was so upset. She just said, "It's only a few videos Ruby. Make some new ones. You got a million hits once, you can do it again."

Ella sent me a DM saying, "Boomer advice. It's the worst !! Listen, that's some serious shade right there Ruby. I'm shook.. like lowkey. I'd be so salty if it was me. That basic bitch is NOT your friend."

Mum said, "Happiness is the best revenge Ruby, just move on and ignore her."

In the end I just started a new channel, but it totally convinced me that I won't EVER trust anything she does again. LIKE EVER.

I told Neville that, but he just said, "LIKE EVEERRRRR" in a really bad American accent and started singing the Taylor Swift song, "We are never ever getting back together." He's the world's BIGGEST idiot .. and WORST singer. Why is he even in a band ???? He's like completely tone deaf. Total embarrassment.

In August the Amazon rainforest was totally on fire! Auntie Ellie was really upset, people are blaming the President for bad environment policies and she just said not enough is happening to stop climate change.

Also some billionaire American paedo is dead. There's loads of news about it .. not sure why.

25th August

Helen's family have moved up North, they are quite a long way from us now. Her boys aren't very happy about it. We just went for a visit this weekend. The dog did about 13k the first night chasing their dog round the house - and we didn't even get there until 8 o'clock at night because the traffic was terrible. It was such a fun weekend. Neville and Mark spent most of the time in the pub and we took the dogs for walks. Mum and Helen drunk a LOT of wine (of course) and talked non-stop. The boys reckon their neighbour is a paedo. Whenever their football goes over the fence he won't give it back and says they have to come round and get it in person. They don't want to go in there, so they keep buying new footballs instead. They said his wife looks like a Choad - we were all giggling about that - Mum had to google what it meant.

We went to this place called Inflatoworld - it was full of inflatable slides and ball pits and stuff - it was good fun, but the whole place absolutely STANK of BO. I think I prefer Bounce with all the trampolines. Helen said her friend's son works at Inflatoworld on the weekends and he found an actual TURD in one of the ball pits last week. Urggh. I think Helen only suggested we did it so her, Neville, Mark and Mum would have an excuse to go to the pub for an hour. Mum said the pub was a bit grim, it looked like a Chinese Take away from the outside and your feet stuck to the floor inside. Mark loves it there and sneaks off there all the time. If he pops out to get fish and chips he's normally gone for 2 hours. They went to another pub the next day that was a really old fashioned one, Mum and Helen were the only two women there. It was full of little old men, all sitting at tables on their own with a pint and paying for beer with loads of coins from little purses. Mum said they didn't seem to know what contactless was and they looked at her like she had just got off a spaceship when she went up to the bar.

The boys are so nervous about starting at a new school - I don't blame them, I wouldn't want to change schools now. I would miss my friends so much. Well not Izzy obviously. I wish SHE would move away so I don't have to look at her annoying face every day !

September 2019

Auntie Ellie spent most of September going on about Greta Thunberg and what a great role model she is. No one else cares. She apparently sailed to a UN meeting so she wouldn't damage the environment - sounded like everyone else flew there on planes (including Ellie!) Greta gave a big speech where she said "I shouldn't be here, I should be at school .... How dare you! You have stolen my dreams and my childhood with your empty words."

This week there were loads of protests round the World by school kids - this was all because of Greta Thunberg. The protests are all complaining that the world leaders aren't addressing the climate crisis and something needs to be done quickly to help save the planet.

Grandpa wanted to know if me or Ella were going to protest. He said, "It won't affect us oldies, but you young people should be taking an interest, it's your future that's at stake."

Ella said, "I think Greta needs to chill a bit."

Uncle John said, "Precisely Ella, Donald Trump said exactly the same thing on Twitter. Told her she had an 'anger management" problem and should chill and go to the Cinema."

Ella agreed and said, "Yeah .. totally. Her and that Malala one .. they should be partying and that. They are well missing out doing all this politics stuff."

Helen's sons started at their new school. It's all boys. Eddie is in year 7 and Henry's in Year 10 like me. He's got a weird pervy form teacher who told them they've all got 'insignificant penises.' Mum said that he shouldn't really be a teacher by the sounds of it. Also Henry said the boy who sits next to him hasn't got a rectum. Eddie said his teacher always has a boner. Our school seems normal and pretty boring compared to theirs....

October 2019

2nd October

Ella has gone off to University. She wasn't bothered about going before, but then she changed her mind. She is in Liverpool doing Media Studies. Grandpa doesn't think that should even be a subject. Seriously .. boomers ! She's having SUCH a great time. She has 5 flatmates and they sound like they are all really good fun. It doesn't sound like she is doing ANY work - they just seem to go to bars all the time - like EVERY night. Whenever I send her messages, she's always got a hangover. She just sends back emojis with sunglasses on or vomit faces and says stuff like, "Can't talk now Ruby ... last night was a well massive bender .. started in 'Spoons at lunchtime .. totally lit. Proper carnage."

28th October

Uncle Dave put Uber on Ella's phone, so if she got separated from her friends at night she'd be able to get home safely and not take the bus on her own. It was just for emergencies, but it was linked to his credit card. Ella worked out she could use the App to get food on Uber Eats, so she got takeaways delivered to their flat 4 nights a week. She paid on the App and got all her flat mates to give her cash, so she was actually making a profit. Uncle Dave has just realised after 4 weeks 'cos he checked his bank statement and said she had to give him all the money back. Except she couldn't, because she said she's spent it all at Wetherspoons.

Neville thought it was funny and said she'd make a business woman yet. Ella said, "I'm not bovvered about all that, I might become an influencer, yeah?"

Grandpa wanted to know, "what on earth she thought she was going to influence?" but she told him he'd never understand it because "Boomers can't relate to the modern world."

He told her that was absolute nonsense and went off toplay a game of bowls.

Also in October Mum randomly became really good friends with Martha Appleby! Of all the people? She was walking the dog one day down by the river and she came across Mrs Appleby sitting on a bench, all by herself, absolutely sobbing. Mum stopped to see if she was OK because she was crying so much, and she basically poured her heart out about how unhappy she was with Mr Appleby (who actually sounds like a bit of a bully). She told Mum that she doesn't feel she can do anything right and she only makes such a fuss over all the kids activities and outfits, and home crafts and everything, because she's trying to prove to him that she's a good mother. He doesn't seem to appreciate anything she does and just complains and belittles her in front of people all the time. He spends most of his time out cycling with his mate Trevor. Mum told her she must concentrate on herself and the kids and that she's doing a fabulous job. Then she started to check in on her most days, because she said lots of people "are fighting battles you can't see and you just need to be kind." I'm sure I've seen that on a meme somewhere. But it's fair enough - I'm glad she has someone to talk to if she's that unhappy. She seems really nice. I know Mum feels really bad that we used to say horrible things about her.

Also Helen got a job at a junior school doing lunch time supervising and serving food. There's a little boy that comes in every day and shouts stuff at her. Stuff like "die dinner lady, DIE !!!" She seems to really like the job, even though she dislikes most of the kids.

November 2019

Venice has TOTALLY flooded ! It normally floods a little bit, but this was the worst it's EVER been. St Mark's Square (which is the famous bit) had to close and some fancy building had like 4 million pounds of water damage. Mum and Neville went there a few years ago for a romantic weekend (vomit). Mum said it's the most beautiful place, with all the little canals and boats and lovely buildings. Neville just muttered something about the cost, but Mum showed me some of her photos of the trip. It really is a pretty place.

Ellie of course started on about Climate Chaos.

Later in November, EVERYONE was on about Prince Andrew. Turns out he was friends with that billionaire paedo guy that died or maybe committed suicide or whatever it was. He was a sex trafficker or that's what it says in the papers and Prince Andrew used to hang out with him at all these parties and stuff!!

This young girl said she was made to have sex with Prince Andrew (who is seriously OLD) there was a photo of them together at this nightclub. He had an interview on the BBC and said that he couldn't possibly have been at the nightclub, because he took Princess Beatrice to a party at the Pizza Express in Woking that evening. There were loads of jokes about it because people in the Royal Family don't go to places like Pizza Express.

The girl also said he was really sweaty, but he said it couldn't have been him because he doesn't sweat. He said he stopped sweating after getting shot at in the Falklands War.

Neville said the interview was the "biggest load of bollocks" he'd ever heard in a very long time and said, "he's made things worse going on TV, absolute car crash, he should have just kept quiet the stupid twat !"

December 2019

Neville says the Tories have called an election in December JUST so they can ruin everyone's Christmas. I'm not sure that's true. Mum says it's because Boris just wants extra support for getting Brexit sorted out finally.

The Conservative's won again anyway and now have loads more seats whatever that means. Neville said it was a 'landslide' and they now have 'a huge majority' so can do whatever they want.

Meanwhile in America they are trying to get rid of Trump. He got impeached whatever that is. Auntie Ellie said it means he should be removed from office, due to committing various crimes and misdemeanors, but that the Senate will most likely let him off. I don't know what the Senate is - their political system sounds even more complicated than ours.

That's what happened in the end, they let him off, so she was right. So for now he's still there. Uncle John was happy. He likes Trump for some reason. He always argues with Auntie Ellie about it and deliberately appears in his 'Make America Great Again' cap whenever we FaceTime just because he knows it annoys her.

Time magazine named Greta Thunberg as the person of the year. Which is a pretty big deal. But Trump thought it should have been him - typical - even though it sounds like he's an actual criminal, he still thinks he's the best at everything.

****

So that's just a bit of stuff that happened last year … back to NOW and 2020.

Everyone is talking about how it's the start of not just a new YEAR but a new DECADE and that 2020 will be brilliant and the most AMAZING year ever. Mum has made a big vision board for her year with all the things she plans to do and places she plans to visit. It's taking up a whole wall in the meditation shed. Or the 'Zen Den' as she calls it. That's annoying.

She said she's just going to focus on her own dreams and not get affected by other people spreading their fake lives on Instagram. I suggested that she just ignore Instagram - she's no good at it for a start (just posts REALLY cringy stuff) and she doesn't even NEED to go on there. She's soooooo obsessed with it … sad really. TikTok is sooo much better - me and Em spent about 2 hours watching really funny videos this morning.

Mum just spent about 2 hours posting this whole 'my 2020 plan' photo album on instagram. What a waste of time … 2 hours. Seriously.

She's added all the places she plans to go. There are yoga weekends and rainforest eco-trips, city breaks in Europe and physical challenges like trekking in the Himalayas and cycling across France …. AS. IF. We don't have the money for all that for one thing, and she literally NEVER rides a bike anywhere and can barely walk upstairs without moaning and groaning .. I can't exactly see her going up actual mountains????? She told me trekking is like hiking and she won't actually be climbing .. either way it'll be tougher than the stairs won't it? So I can't see that happening somehow.

Oh and we've got a 'swear jar' now. It's pretty much ENTIRELY aimed at Neville to be honest. Mum said any money we get from it will go towards some nice family days out and trips away. Let's see if it makes any difference at all. He doesn't like giving money away so it might actually work. But I’m kind of hoping it doesn’t so we can plan some nice trips this year.

2nd January

So the whole "concentrating on her own dreams' thing didn't last long .. Mum is STILL jealous of ABSOLUTELY everything Jasmine does !! Right now she is at a luxury resort in Sri Lanka on a "bespoke yoga and wellness detoxing experience." Her insta-feed is totally packed with stunning images of her doing yoga poses by jungle streams, and floating in an AMAZING infinity pool. She is eating something called an "Ayurvedic Vegetarian" diet. It's designed especially for her and it "rebalances the doshas, encourages energy stimulation and calms the mind." What on earth is a dosha?? Who cares .. I just love looking at all her amazing pictures on Insta. Mum still doesn't know I follow Jasmine so I always try to sound vague when she talks about where she is and what she's doing.

Mum said, "Listen to her going on about her special cleansing diet. Honestly - talk about pretentious." Then she made a big song and dance of making a green juice in the new juicer that she got for Christmas. She ORDERED Neville to buy it for her so she could start the new year with a totally different 'food mindset' and because juice cleanses are fantastic for 'clarity and energy.' It will be interesting to see how often she uses it … my guess is it will end up covered in dust, cluttering up the worktop within 2 weeks.

Anyway, Jasmine's photos are soooooo amazing! She is staying in a suite where the bedroom part is totally MASSIVE. The bedroom overlooks the jungle and has this enormous 4-poster bed covered in draped mosquito nets.

Then there's a massive patio area that faces the mountains, with an outdoor bathroom with a huge rainfall shower and massive oval bath. She posted a picture lying in this bath and it had been filled with rose petals … there was all this mist coming from the mountains behind her … it was really atmospheric. She even has her own infinity pool and outdoor bed if she wants to sleep under the stars.

SOOOOOO AMAZING !

To be fair we actually had an infinity pool and a bathroom that was outside at one of our Airbnb's in Bali - there was a tree growing through the middle of the bathroom and the whole shower bit of the room didn't have a roof .. it was pretty cool. Apart from getting bitten by insects. You could hear all these jungle noises like frogs and those things that make a clicking noise…

The resort where Jasmine is staying is just soooooo exotic. OMG I would LOVE to stay somewhere like that one day. Me and Em were talking about it, we decided that we need, like, a really successful YouTube channel or we will have to get TikTok famous, so we can just travel the world and stay where we want.

Mum keeps muttering, "Well I've been doing yoga for much longer than her - she must have got the idea from me telling her about my Bali retreat." Trust her to think that! Turns out this fancy resort contacted Jasmine direct and invited her for free so she could promote it on her blog. And they paid for the flight.

Neville said, "your mother reading Jasmine's blog again is she? Seriously, it's like actually performing psychological torture on yourself."

Mum said, "shut up Neville" and dragged me into the garden to take a photo of her in a yoga "tree pose" with the only bit of the garden that looks semi-decent in the background. Then she dragged me back out there later on and tried to do a "dancer's pose," because Jasmine had just posted an amazing example of this exact pose, in silhouette, against a PERFECT sunset. Jasmine is super flexible and REALLY good at yoga.

I tried to tell Mum it would look really sh*t doing it in our garden (and not against a beautiful sunset) and she should just stop trying to compete. It didn't really matter in the end since she's pretty rubbish at yoga. She wobbled really badly about 4 times and then completely fell over and smashed her knee on the lawnmower, which Neville had left in the middle of the lawn.

So then she got angry with Neville yelling "Why have you left that there....?" And he yelled back " Where do you suggest I put it ??? You've filled the whole shed to bursting point with all your spiritual junk !!!" If you want my opinion he was in the right, but she went off into a sulk for the rest of the night anyway.

Honestly!! And people say teenagers are moody. They have nothing on jealous menopausal mothers.

3rd January

Dry January is going well. Both Mum and Neville have massive hangovers.

4th January

Mum seems to have got over her bad mood about Jasmine. The fact that Debbie's family are all going through their first winter vomiting bug of the new year seems to have cheered her up no end.

She's been rattling on about booking a skiing holiday for half-term since it's something she has never done, and it's important to "challenge yourself by trying out new things." Neville told her if she wants to try a new thing, she could try earning more money - especially if she plans to go off on holiday 'willy nilly.' He hasn't said that for a while. It made me smile.

Feels like FOREVER since we've been on holiday - it would be lovely to go away for half term. I doubt that we will though .. we don't usually. We are going to Dorset at Easter and there are two bedrooms so Em's coming with us again to keep me company, which is really cool. Neville wants to go to the Jurassic coast (don't know what that is), but it should be fun taking the idiot dog to the beach. She's never been. We were going to take her for a weekend before, but in the end we decided not to - it was more relaxing without her to be honest. The place we were staying had chickens next door so it's a good job we didn't … she'd have been through the fence terrorising them.

She once got through the fence at a neighbours house while we were in their garden having a cup of tea and a chat. The neighbours said the fence was completely safe as their dog couldn't fit through it anywhere, but ours managed to find a tiny gap and squeeze through. They had chickens in a coop at the end of the garden and she didn't notice to start with, we were calling her back when she suddenly noticed them, shot straight towards them and managed to grab hold of one of them. Neville leapt over the fence (actually the most athletic thing I have EVER seen him do) and shouted "drop the f***ing chicken, NOW!! DROP IT," in a really menacing voice. The dog was just standing there .. looking totally gormless, with a flapping scared-looking chicken wedged in it's mouth. Neville screamed, "I said NOW … DROP THAT." The dog suddenly looked worried, spat the chicken out and ran in the nearest bush. Neville clambered into the bush and dragged her out. The poor chicken limped back to the end of the garden, really slowly, shaking with fear. It was so embarrassing, and I felt so, so sorry for the poor chicken. It probably has PTSD.

5th January

Talking about skiing - it turns out Jake is skiing with his family, their flight got cancelled so he won't be back at school for a few days. His Mum has banned him from using his phone whilst they are away because they are having "quality time as a family." OMG .. that must be soooooo boring. They probably have to talk to each other in the evenings ….

Martha Appleby was round today for a lunchtime drink with Mum. They chat for HOURS now when they get together - if it's after school they start with tea but it normally turns into wine about 5pm, when one of them says "sun's over the yardarm" or similar. She wanted to know if I could babysit next Friday night. I've done loads of babysitting for them since her and Mum became friends. It's a pretty easy way to earn money - I'd love to do more of it really. I need to find some more people that need a babysitter. I asked Mum for some advice, but she just said, "I had to find my own jobs at your age Ruby, use your imagination." So that wasn't very helpful.

They finished their G&Ts and Mum said, "Are you rushing off or shall we open the wine?" and Martha replied, "You know what? To hell with it, yes, lets. Terence can sort the kids out for once. He probably won't even notice I'm not there, Trevor was over so they were squashed on the sofa with the laptop ordering more skin-tight lycra cycling gear .. as if they don't have tons already .. they get matching stuff too, they look like a right pair of idiots."

Later on I came out of my room to sort some food out since Mum and Martha were on their second or third bottle and there was no sign of ANY dinner being cooked for me. They had bags of crisps, and twiglets and jars of pickles open all over the kitchen island and were cackling away about something or other. I put some pizza in the oven and went back to my room. When I went back to get it out of the oven Martha was shouting into her phone, "No Terence, I'm NOT coming home now. I will be back when I FEEL LIKE IT. Get off your lycra-clad arse, and put the kids to bed yourself."

She slammed the phone down violently on the worktop and Mum cheered and they high-fived one another. I wouldn't be surprised if Martha just smashed her phone screen, but the two of them were too happy to notice.

6th January

School was a nightmare. First day back always is, but it was even worse because EVERYONE has iPhoneXs or worse iPhone11s.

Mum said I was being ridiculous and it's impossible that EVERYONE has one. She just doesn't get it. At least now phones are banned for most of the school day, so I don't have to look at them so much. I still have to see a ton of pictures on Insta and Snapchat though. The camera is really amazing, which just means Izzy is taking EVEN MORE selfies, if that is even possible ! So annoying. Still … she is SO not my problem anymore. Since we all stopped speaking to her she's been hanging out with Maisie and Megan or The "Ms" as they STILL like to call themselves. They all deserve each other to be honest. Neville calls them "Ignorant Izzy and the M's" - he was pleased with that - he thinks it sounds like a really shit old-fashioned girl band.

Seriously. Sad.

I sort of missed Jake at school actually. Obviously he's not my boyfriend anymore, but he's not Izzy's either! We still get on OK - and he makes me laugh in Maths so it was boring without him. I don't "LIKE" like him anymore. I think Izzy thinks I do … maybe I will try to get back with him JUST to annoy her !

Mum spent the whole of dinner this evening talking about her friend Mary - she's worse than Mum for doing weird stuff and dressing in strange outfits. Her daughter Lucy is in my year and people call her Luna Lovegood as a joke because she floats about looking really vague all the time and always drifts off in class when she has to answer a question. Mum was saying, "I think Mary's approach to things is so good. She doesn't believe in rules or strict routines … they make sure they communicate as a whole family, but they do it equally using a talking stick." Neville caught my eye when she said that and we both giggled. "They work around rhythms that everyone in the house has to "feel into". There's no fixed agenda or timings .. it's wonderful."

I said it's also probably the reason Lucy is late for school EVERY day.

9th January

Jake's back. And he's tanned. He's SOOOOO fit. We didn't talk to each other, but he smiled at me at break and sent me 2 messages. I didn't think I still liked him. In fact I was SURE I didn't, but now I really want him to be my boyfriend again …..and not JUST to annoy Izzy. Arghghghghgh !!!

10th January

I babysat for Archie and Alice Appleby tonight. I always used to think they were really spoilt, but that was before before Mum got to know Martha properly. They are really sweet funny little kids. We usually play games and I let them watch a bit of TV and they always go to bed when they are supposed to. Martha always leaves me nice cakes and biscuits to eat and the wifi code (obviously) so it's not exactly a tough job. They usually go to the pub or out for a meal and they come back a bit drunk, so Mr Appleby always gives me far too much money.

When I got there Mr Appleby "call me Terence" was pacing up and down the lounge and Mrs Appleby was finishing off getting dressed. She'd done her hair really nicely and had a lovely outfit on and her make up looked so nice as well. She said, "How do I look Terence?" smiling at him. He barely looked at her and replied, "you look like you always do Martha, now get a move on the table's booked for 7.00."

She looked really sad so I said, "I think you look very pretty Martha, that lipstick's a really cool shade."

When Mum came to collect me later, she kind of did a half whisper, half hiss thing, so Terence couldn't hear, and said to Martha, "how was it?". She just replied, "same as ever" and looked really tearful. Then she put on a fake happy voice and said, "Thanks so much Ruby, see you soon," as she waved goodbye.

11th January

Mum wasn't around when I got up this morning - Neville said she'd gone to have a cosmic reading to find out about the energy of 2020 - that sounded totally like the kind of weird rubbish she would be stupid enough for pay for.

He looked pretty rough. Probably hungover. Chemical Banana played at the Working Men's Club last night, which would explain the state of him. Apparently they've been trying out a couple of "original" songs rather than just playing all covers. I bet THAT was a treat for everyone.

When I asked Neville how it went and he said, "Well we played to a sell out crowd of 7.. which included Mad Brenda who does the meat raffle. I was hoping there'd be a bit of a buzz, but to be honest we got a pretty lukewarm response to our latest song "Margarine and Radiators."

I tried to sound encouraging and say that not many people go out in January because they've used all their money at Christmas, but I'm not sure if it helped or not.

Mum was in a good mood when I got home. She said her reading was amazing - apparently there was some kind of eclipse yesterday which was followed by a Saturn-Pluto conjunction in the sign of Capricorn. I learnt about conjunctions in year 6 for my SATs exams, but I've forgotten it all !! Also I don't suppose it's the same kind of conjunction. The energy reader woman told Mum that this kind of "cosmic alignment" is extremely rare and carries life-changing, transformative energy that will shape the whole year.

Mum's now even more convinced that this will be the most amazing year ever …. I hope she is right…..

She's re-watching that Kon Marie show on Netflix and rattling on about decluttering things that don't spark joy again. She keeps saying stuff like .. "well of course I've been following the Kon Marie method for years.."

Neville isn't happy. LOADs of people have watched it now and so THEY are all decluttering, which means that Mum is just buying up loads of cheap pointless junk on the local sales sites. I just heard him shouting, "f**k sake Jaz, what was the point of you getting rid of all that stuff I actually liked, just to replace it with a load of ugly crap someone else is chucking out? Where's the Joy?"

Oh .. speaking of which Mum ended up ditching "CREATIVITY" as her word of the year last year and going back to "JOY" .... yeah right! To be honest, her and Neville argued more than EVER last year, so there wasn't exactly much joy around. In the end they went to some couples' counsellor and now they talk about their feelings, and kiss in front of me - it's disgusting..... I don't know what's worse to be honest !! I think I preferred the rows.

Ever since new years eve Mum's been banging on about choosing this year's word. She's finally decided - apparently it's going to be FREEDOM !! She is going to find ways to be totally free in all aspects of her life and not "constrained by rules and expectations" or tied to the way "society" and "the patriarchy" expect her to live her life.

I don't know what "the patriarchy" is ....she started to explain what it meant, which was mostly banging on about how modern women don't need men and shouldn't have to put up with old value systems that give men the advantage and keep women in subservient roles. She said "us Feminists want to be independent and pay our own way." I changed the subject by reminding her she needed to get changed because Neville wanted to take her out to dinner.

Then she said, "it had better be his treat, I'm not going halves." So much for Feminists .....

12th January

There is giggling and cuddling going on in the kitchen this morning - yuk!

Must mean they had a nice evening. Mum said it was lovely. He'd chosen a really romantic little restaurant they hadn't been to before - there were candles on the table and posh wine. She said it was like when they were first dating and they should do it more often. She told me the couples' Counsellor said "lots of couples do a date night every week to ensure they find time for one another and rekindle the spark between them."

Neville started to say, "EVERY week?" in a bit of a pissed off voice, and Mum shot him one of her looks, so he carried on, "every week sounds like a really nice plan Jaz - yeah let's have a think about that."

Mum went off upstairs to get dressed and he said, "blimey Ruby, I'm not shelling out for a fancy dinner every week - spark or no spark. It cost me an arm and a leg last night."

I just spent about 2 hours trying to do physics homework. I don't understand any of it. What's the point of physics .... seriously???

14th January

Mum has been working a few hours part-time at Ollie's vegan cafe. She says she's not getting enough graphic design work at the moment because of Brexit [eyeroll]. I said it's more likely that loads of people can do logo designs themselves or buy them on Etsy, but she said that was nonsense. Then she said, "anyway I don't just make logos, I create the entire brand concept from the ground up." I dunno what the ground has to do with any of it. Either way she needed another part-time job.

Anyway .. there's a bit of a drama going on in the work WhatsApp group and the phone has been pinging constantly for the last half hour - I've told her it's annoying and she should switch the notifications off. She said she needs to have them on in case of important work information. It's more likely because she's nosy - two of the staff have fallen out, they used to go out with each other, but then one of them cheated and now they now want to work at different branches, but it's too complicated with all the staff and working out the different shifts fairly. So they are stuck there together and they are arguing about everything and not getting any work done.

And I thought school was full of drama!

Ollie isn't Neville's boss anymore .. this bloke called Keith Kitchen is his boss - that always makes me laugh. Ollie left at Christmas to run the Vegan cafe full time and he's planning on opening 2 more cafes nearby because it's going so well. It's also a "remote work space," so it's always full of people on laptops with big headphones. Mum used to take her laptop there sometimes and do design stuff, but she said it's not the same now she works there because she gets distracted if a table needs tidying or she feels like she should be helping out if there's a big queue.

Neville likes that fact she works there, because he can still be mean about Ollie. I like the fact she works there, because I sometimes get the old cake that's being thrown out. The caramel slices are the best - they taste really nice even though they are vegan.

She likes it there, but she can't do the fancy patterns on the coffee very well so she just tells people that it's abstract art or claims they are something they aren't - like she'll say it's a butterfly or a leaf when it's just a blob and they usually nod awkwardly and say … "oh yes… I can see it now .."

Neville still manages to upset her though. She said he should be encouraging the fact she's doing something new, instead of criticising and making fun of her.

But he just walked in and said, "how's your latte art coming on then Jaz? Are all your designs still looking like deformed testicles?"

16th January

Mum and I had to go to Tescos today - she wanted to go to the big Tesco for some reason instead of getting a delivery. Turned out to be quite exciting as there was a big drama when we were queuing to pay. This woman pushed a massive trolley full of stuff through the till in front of us and then ran off, and her friend pretended to faint to create a diversion, the security men had tried to chase the other woman out to the carpark but lost her, so they'd come and back and were telling the one by the till to get up or they'd call the police and arrest her. They were trying to take her purse off of her so she could pay for the trolley load that had just been stolen. It was really exciting. Shopping is usually really boring. Unless I'm buying stuff for me.

The woman on the till said, "I dunno … It's all been going on in here today … it's the 3rd time the security men have kicked off." She told us there were these 2 blokes in earlier, who were walking around the shop just eating loads of stuff so they didn't need to pay for any of it. She said they ate 2 whole chickens on the way round, and the security men saw it on the store cameras.

We were telling Neville when we got home and Mum said it must have been those whole roasted ones since neither of them looked like Alice Cooper. I said, "Who's she?" And Neville said, "HE Ruby, HE is a rock star - and he didn't EAT an uncooked chicken Jaz, he just threw one off the stage. And that killed it, well I think so .. or someone threw it at him and that killed it .. or something like that. Anyway, you're thinking of Ozzy Osbourne - he's the one that ate the head off of a bat.

I told him not to be so ridiculous ….. he really is SUCH an idiot .. people don't eat things like bats.

Also, I wanted to know what's wrong with all these people they keep talking about. Stars like Lewis Capaldi and Ed Sheeren don't carry on like that nowadays. Neville just muttered, "It was mostly the excessive use of mind bending drugs Ruby - it's a miracle either of them are still alive to be honest."

17th January

There's some stuff on the news about a scary virus in China - turns out it might have been caused by someone eating a BAT !!!

So weird after our conversation we had yesterday …. They are saying it's a bit like bad flu, but MUCH more dangerous because people LITERALLY can't breathe and it's killing LOADS of people in China. They have actually blocked off a whole city to try and stop it - everyone in hospitals has to wear all this weird plastic protective clothing, like out of a Sci-Fi film and people can't leave their houses or go to school or do anything. It's called the Coronavirus. Neville just said, "Oh, like the beer."

At least it's far away, so it won't be a problem for us.

I still think it's kind of amazing that anyone would want to eat a bat ….. But I sometimes watch travel programmes with Neville and there are some really strange things on menus in other countries. I don't even like weird stuff like liver .. Mum loves it .. although not at the moment because she's insisting she's still a vegan. She's not.

18th January

We went to London to look after Coco and Felix for the weekend. Auntie Sophie and Uncle Mark went on a mini-break. We took them to the Natural History Museum because Felix likes dinosaurs. Coco said she loved the museum, but that the ride on The Tube was a bit laborious. We were all impressed by that, especially Neville who said HE doesn't use words that big .. even in work meetings.

When I was helping Coco put her pyjamas on I noticed a word of the day flip-chart in her room. It has words like astonished, turbulent, incessant and dilapidated on it. She said, "it's to improve my vocabulary." Perhaps I should get one … it might impress my English teacher.

Coco had the class bear for the weekend - just like when I was at school - some of the stuff in the book was really impressive, because the Mums had got REALLY competitive. Neville said, "sod that, we'll just take it to a couple of fast food outlets."

19th January

When we got back from London Mum made a big fuss about making us roast dinner. She did me a special bit of lamb.

When she served up theirs Neville said, "WTF Jaz .. it's a cauliflower."
She said, "it's a ROAST."
He said, "it's a f***ing CAULIFLOWER, where's the rest of my dinner?"

20th January

Mum wasn't at the cafe today. She said she spent the whole day on the sofa binge-watching The Crown on Netflix - she keeps telling me boring facts about the Royals. I don't really care. I like Harry and Megan, but that's about it. And George 'cos he seems really naughty.

Neville just told Mum they've announced that Gillian Anderson will be playing Margaret Thatcher in season 4 of The Crown - he said there were lots of things on twitter with the hashtag #awkward boner … I don't know who Gillian Anderson is …. and I really don't want to ask after he mentioned boners .. why can't they have these conversations in private ?

I had to leave the room.

21st January

Mum just got in from a long shift at the cafe and just told me off for binge-watching Friday Night Dinner. Typical … it's all very well for her to lie around watching TV. I was about to complain, but she suddenly burst into tears for no reason and ran upstairs.

Neville just rolled his eyes, got a beer out of the fridge and said "Menopause."

I don’t know if that’s what it is or not … she definitely cries more often and spends a lot of time in bed. She did that a lot last year, I think she was depressed, but she didn’t want to talk about it. It’s why she started running (or trying to run) because being outside getting a bit of exercise really helped her feel happier. Some days she didn’t even get out of bed or get dressed so she must have had something wrong with her. She seems a bit better now, but some days she does seem really sad.

She reappeared a bit later, but then didn’t even make dinner. She said, “I can’t even think about food. I’ve spent the whole day smashing avocados onto Sourdough. I’m over it Ruby.” Then she grabbed two bags of crisps and a curly wurly and went to bed saying, “I’ve downloaded a meditation webinar and I need to work through it in peace.”

Neville went out and got us takeaway pizza and we watched Call the Midwife on the iplayer. It’s really nice - it’s about the old days in London, but it’s really sad in places too. Grandma always watches it, but I never bothered until recently.

25th January

Cathie & Richard came to stay for the weekend and brought their dog Derek with them. Last time we stayed with them Derek killed a sparrow when we took the dogs for a walk and then he carried it around with him for the whole weekend. I think he was protecting it from our stupid dog, but to be honest she really wasn’t interested in it .. she was more interested in watching Cathie make us a roast dinner, hoping she’d get some scraps. Cathie said that Derek carried the dead sparrow around for at least a week after we left. Finally it’s head fell off, so they took it off him.

They are all in the kitchen having G&Ts and Cathie was saying, “well that’s nothing .. a few weeks ago he took down a badger!!”

So the story went that Derek found this badger hole or "sett" - Neville insisted on correcting Cathie whilst she was trying to tell the story ..[eyeroll]. He's watched a couple of David Attenborough documentaries and suddenly he's a wildlife expert.

So Derek went scuttling down there and just wouldn't come out. Richard went and got a torch from home and shined it down there so they could see what was going on. Derek was just sitting there, with this massive dead badger. He wouldn't come back out again, because he wanted to guard his kill. Cathie was trying to coax him out with cheese and bits of sausage and everything .... and in the end Richard had to actually crawl into the tunnel and drag Derek out by his legs. But it was hard for Richard to crawl backwards whilst dragging out Derek, so Cathie had to hold onto Richard's feet and pull him out, while he pulled Derek out ...

She said it was just off the path to this nice country pub, so they ended up with this big audience of dog walkers and people going for Sunday lunch, a couple of kids were filming it on their phones. They got him out eventually and put him on the lead. Then it took the two of him to drag him away. They don't do that dog walk anymore.

Luckily Richard is really thin, so he managed to get in pretty easily. Neville started joking about trying to get HIS beer belly into a badger's sett. I can just imagine him getting wedged into a tunnel and someone having to actually DIG him back out ... it would be like in the Winnie the Pooh story where he eats too much food at Rabbit's house and gets stuck in the hole when he tries to leave, but they can't pull him out so he has to stay there for a week until he gets thin again.

27th January

The M's and Izzy had a party on Saturday, but hardly anyone turned up. They aren't happy. They ended up getting drunk and doing loads of embarrassing TikToks .. mostly them dancing around with bottles and falling over. They ended up deleting some of them, but loads of people had already seen them. Maisie drank so much she was really sick all day yesterday .. she's not even in school today so it must have been bad. We were giggling about some of the videos in the canteen at lunch - I think Izzy might have guessed because she kept shooting us horrible looks. I'm so glad she doesn't hang out with us anymore ... all she ever did was talk about herself. It's more fun without her.

Mum came home all happy - she'd had lunch with Martha, Bridget and Jane. They can take time off when they want because they all work for themselves, except for Martha who doesn't have a job. Mr Appleby likes her to be able to keep the house perfect and make nice dinners for him. Mum says he's "living in the dark ages" and "she's not a 1950s housewife," whatever that means.

Martha's been doing much more stuff for herself since her and Mum made friends. Lunch was in the pub and turned into a wine-filled afternoon judging by how "jolly" Mum is being. Mum said Terence Appleby sent about 10 text messages demanding to know why Martha wasn't at home doing the ironing. Mum said, "I have no idea how she puts up with it. He's horrible to her, just orders her around and doesn't pay her any attention at all. Barely notices her. She could dye her hair purple and he wouldn't notice. He only notices when the house is messy. I know they go on date nights - they've been doing those since I referred her to the couples' counsellor we used. I thought getting some therapy might help them, but they seem to be growing further and further apart. Poor Martha. It's one thing to be lonely if you are single, but there's nothing worse than feeling lonely when you are actually in a relationship with someone Ruby."

Then she wobbled off to have a soak in the bath.

I think I might become a couples' counsellor. Seems like all you do is tell people to go on a date night and they pay you 65 quid an hour.

30th January

APPARENTLY Brexit is about to happen tomorrow .. but they've said that before. I don't really even know what that means, but then neither does anyone else apparently - not even Boris and he's supposed to be sorting it out. He just keeps talking about "oven ready" deals. It's fair to say there has been a lot of ranting in our house about it. Neville says that Boris is "just a posh useless twat that lies about everything, hides in fridges when the going gets tough and spaffs money up the wall." I don't know what "spaffing" is, but it seems a bit weird that a Prime Minister would hide in a fridge …. must have been a big one .. he's not very slim.

So ONE MONTH into 2020 and things really haven't started that well to be honest ….. there's climate change chaos, political drama and record numbers of people using food banks. Most of Australia is ON FIRE, because it's been so hot and they've had NO rain. There are massive bush fires everywhere and Koala's dying all over the place - which is really really sad. The photos on the news are terrible. Trump is trying to cause lots of trouble and start a war and everyone is STILL going on about Brexit ALL the time.

Things are pretty tough for the Queen too, since all that stuff came out about Prince Andrew being a paedo !! To be honest she doesn't seem too bothered about that, she's more upset that Harry and Megan don't want to be in the Royal Family anymore.

Me and Mum popped to see Grandma and Grandpa today after school and Ella popped round to say hello as well. Grandma had bought some mini battenbergs. Grandpa was reading the paper, shaking his head and tutting.

He likes a good tut.

He said, "It's a bloody nonsense. Our media actually think Prince Harry and that actress woman are more important than the political situation in the Middle East or the potential economic ramifications of Brexit."

I don't know what a ramification is …. but he seemed unhappy about it.

My Cousin Ella thinks Harry and Megan are really great. Ella changed her name to Shanequa a couple of years ago, but after a while she decided it was a bit stupid and changed it back again. Grandma and Grandpa thought it was pretty stupid all along and only ever called her Ella so they didn't really notice when she made a big thing about changing it back.

She just said, "you don't get it Grandpa, it's like they are, like, following their own path yeah? 'Cos being a Royal is like being in an institution that's well, like, totally not modern anymore yeah? I think they are leaving because Megan is well woke."

He replied, "Woke? What are you talking about? Do you mean awake ? Honestly you come out with some rubbish my girl." And Grandma said, "Stop saying "like" every other word Ella. You need to learn to talk properly. It's all this bloody texting you young people do, it's stopping your ability to communicate."

2nd February

Today is 02 02 2020 …. Apparently it's a Palindrome.

Grandpa put it on the family WhatsApp and said, "This is the first global palindrome day for 909 years, which incidentally is ALSO a palindrome." There wasn't much of a response to start with .. no-one seems to care apart from him. Although Uncle Dave posted a GIF of some tumbleweed. So then Grandma commented.

Grandma: That's very interesting Jack.
Ella: Yeah Grandpa …. Is that like a parallelogram?
Grandpa: No it isn't Ella - honestly!
Ella: Well, I dunno do I? I was useless at Maths, even though my teacher was called Mr Measure. I love that. Mr Measure! So funny.

I put a smiley face on, but that seemed to be the end of the conversation.

Well I thought that was the end of it until Mum came floating indoors from her meditation shed saying she'd been connecting with her higher self. ** This usually means she'd googled some nonsense about energetic fields and spiritual guides.

She said, "today's date is a really powerful one. It carries magic vibrations, it's all about the feminine creative energies of manifestation. 0202 2020 is a mirror image date Ruby .. it's a gateway where we can look at the rituals we use to nurture our best selves. examine our vibrations and REALLY see what we need to change in our reality."

Whatever. My reality is that Jake just wants to be mates. Izzy is the most annoying person in the world (I have no idea how she was EVER my friend) and tomorrow I have a chemistry test. If Mum has some MAGIC way to change that reality then I'd love to hear it.

5th February

It's Neville's birthday.

I got him a brilliant card .. it said,"I think you're a Bellend, but Mum said I had to get you a card anyway."

I don't really think he's a Bellend. Well. Not all the time. Most of the time he's just an annoying idiot. So is Mum.

We've all been watching Gavin and Stacey loads so Mum got him a Nessa card. It said "I won't lie, you're not everyone's cup of tea, but at the end of the day, when all's said and done, you're tidy. I means it."

They went out for dinner as well. Mum said she'd found a fabulous "Asian Fusion" restaurant with a wonderful range of Vegan options. He didn't look too impressed tbh. He probably doesn't know what Asian Fusion is anyway. I know I don't.

I asked Grandpa. He said, "what a bloody nonsense, what's wrong with proper food." That didn't really help. I should have asked Auntie Sophie, she probably knows, but she's usually really busy and can't always answer messages.

Honestly - I LOVE birthdays, but they don't seem to care. Must be something to do with getting old. Well I say "they" don't care .. Mum does .. she makes a right song and dance about her birthday and drags it out for weeks.

7th February

Philip Schofield came out on TV today. He made a tearful speech about it on This Morning whilst Holly held his hand … I don't know why he had to make a big deal about it. I can't imagine anyone cares. I said as much at dinner, but Neville said, "well I dare say his wife cares."

9th February

Neville just got in the from the pub completely soaking wet, swearing a lot and saying that it's absolutely "wanging it down outside." Storm Ciara is absolutely raging right now and the dog is currently in hiding upstairs. She looked a bit scared earlier, but not scared enough to go off her food ... she got hold of a pack of raw sausages when Mum opened the fridge, and managed to eat half of them before we wrestled them off her.

She probably won't even be sick. She can literally eat ANYTHING. A bit like Neville.

There was just an enormous crash outside. Our neighbour's trampoline just flew across their fence and wedged itself in a big tree two gardens down!

Mum is looking at the internet every five minutes and panicking. She says there's a tornado warning in Cambridgeshire, rivers bursting their banks in Yorkshire, there's flooding all over the place and loads of people with the Coronavirus are being bused into quarantine in Milton Keynes. Loads of flights are cancelled too. Jasmine is raging on instagram, because she's supposed to be appearing on Loose Women tomorrow and can't get home from her luxury skiing weekend. Bridget on the other hand is also stranded on her holiday, because EasyJet have cancelled all their flights, but she really doesn't care at all. She's delighted to have 2 more days in the sunshine drinking cocktails and shopping.

The Family WhatsApp is going crazy and pinging away literally every few seconds. Grandma is in a right state about the storm .. one of their fence panels just came down. But Uncle John is making fun of all of us because where he lives in America they have proper tornados, like on the Wizard of Oz, and they have to hide in special reinforced rooms or lie in the bath to protect themselves. He said over here there's a bit of flooding and a few branches on the railway lines and everyone carries on like it's the apocalypse.

Auntie Ellie is ranting on about it all being because of climate change .. well, when she isn't going on and on about President Trump avoiding impeachment that is. Ella is REALLY annoying Grandpa by saying "wot's impeaching all about? I dunno wot that is."

Grandpa was pretty annoyed already tbh .. he's been complaining ALL DAY about the news being "monopolised by that Schofield bloke coming out of the closet." He wanted to know why "everyone's gay all of a sudden." I told him it isn't EVERYONE, but he just keeps saying it's a bloody nonsense and that it isn't proper NEWS. To be honest I agree with that part. Being gay shouldn't even BE on the news. Mum says there are LOADS of really nasty comments on Twitter. I don't know why anyone would want to be horrible about it really. I like Philip Schofield. Him and Holly are really funny together.

Oh ! Apparently Boris finally "did" Brexit the other day. It really wasn't that big a deal in the end. A few people celebrated in Parliament Square .. no-one really noticed. Neville said, "that Bellend Farage talked a load of crap as usual, a few people waved flags and some fat bloke in a Union Jack t-shirt went viral."

Well at least that's the last we'll hear about it !

11th February

So me and Neville took the idiot dog out for a walk.
Someone walked past and said to Neville, "Aww she's sweet. What is she?"
He replied "A right twat." I think they meant what breed!
I went home before him as the dog just kept stopping to poo and I got really bored.

Neville got back about 20 minutes later looking really angry. He said to Mum, "those bloody raw sausages took their toll on her guts. She did 4 absolutely MASSIVE sh*ts. I ran out of poo bags .. had to pick the last turd up using my Tesco Club Card and try and hoof it in the bin. It was a hell of a lot slimier than it looked ... had to abandon the f**king card."

Mum looked disgusted and Neville added, "I'd have left it there to be honest, but bloody Doreen walked past and was watching me like a hawk. If she hadn't seen me pick it up it'd be all over that bloody FB community page."

The virus thing in China is getting worse. It said on the news that there are now loads of people on Cruise ships that have got it and it's getting really bad in Italy too and starting to spread around. Everyone is wearing masks and things - I don't think it's anything for us to worry about though, but it's not very nice for all the people in those countries. Mum says it's probably because people in Italy are kissing all the time, and walk around holding hands. We don't really do that here. They even kiss the people in shops that give them bread and coffee and stuff. Imagine doing that in Aldi .. I don't think so.

14th February

Valentine's Day.
I hate it.
Same thing every year.

I never get a card from anyone (not even the annoying boy in the year below that has a crush on me).

I didn't even get one last year when I had an ACTUAL boyfriend because Jake didn't think I'd want one - he sent me a cute text instead.

James 2 asked Connor, to ask me, if he could give me a card a couple of days ago. Soooooo embarrassing - I don't even like James 2. I was a bit surprised so I just said, "Errrrr, well I don't really know. Maybe not." I guess that worked because I didn't get a card from him either.

Mum was ranting as usual about “hallmark holidays” whatever they are and “commercial nonsense that makes you feel inadequate and not good enough, especially if you are single.” She said, “Self-love is the most important thing there is and it’s the only love you really need on Valentine’s Day.” Neville said, “Well that’s proper b*llocks Jaz, if that was true there wouldn’t be a multi-million pound industry pushing cards, flowers, chocolates, teddy bears and goodness knows what else every sodding February.”

Mum’s got a new facebook friend called Sophie that sells diet shakes. She has just posted "I need 5 girls to respond. Drop me a heart for every kilo you want to lose this Valentines day."

Mum's always saying stuff like "no-one outside of yourself is responsible for your happiness"; "It all starts with you .. YOU have to love and accept YOU first and then you'll find true inner peace" and "buying a card once a year isn't necessary to show someone how much you love them."

Except it obviously is ...

She's currently shouting at Neville because he posted a screenshot of a Valentine card on her facebook timeline instead of buying her an actual card. It's the thought that counts and he DID get her a really big box of Maltesers.

My WhatsApp just pinged. He's sent me one as well. And it's from the dog which is kind of cute.

After all that it turns out Mum didn't get him anything AT ALL. I just heard her yelling "Alexa ... put “buy Neville some Valentine's Beers,” on the shopping list."

15th February

Mum ordered a really expensive box of diet shakes from Sophie. Apparently they taste disgusting and make her feel sick. Sophie said they are non-refundable, but to stick with it because you get used to the taste. Neville's really angry about the money.

We were supposed to go to Norfolk for the weekend with Suzie so the idiot could play with their dog Ernie on the beach, but there's another storm so no-one wants to drive.

I wish we'd gone. We will all be stuck indoors annoying each other. Mum and Neville are still arguing about the shakes. Mum said, "But the before and after photos are amazing, look Neville," and he said, "Jesus Jaz .. if that's the same woman then my before and afters would look like me and Tom f***ing Hardy."

The storm is called Dennis.
That's a crap name.

16th February

I'm so bored of storms and rain - it's so shit !

Today was just horrible …….. Caroline Flack off of Love Island killed herself yesterday. It's soooooooooooo sad.

Everyone's talking about it and blaming the papers and internet trolls and stuff like that. There were horrible headlines about her - must have been so upsetting for her to see them. She was really depressed too, it sounds like. I don't really know what to say. Mum and Neville have been going on about it for hours and hours and Mum's arguing with Auntie Ellie about the role of the media and something to do with her having to go to court. I don't know what they are on about. I had to ask Em who said it was something about her having a big fight with her boyfriend and getting arrested. People don't really know what was going on in someone's life though so it's really unfair to put horrible things in the paper. We don't even know if any of it was true.

After a while they stopped arguing about Caroline Flack and started arguing about Harry and Megan. And racism. And them being forced out of the country by the right wing press.

I can't see how everyone arguing makes anything better, especially when Mum's whole instagram is full of quotes about being kind. She's even changed her facebook profile to say "Be kind, everyone's fighting a battle you know nothing about."

#BEKIND is everywhere right now. Everyone's doing it because of Caroline Flack. What's the point if you are just going to carry on being mean to people?? A hashtag doesn't mean anything at all ! Mum's not very kind to Neville most of the time. Mind you he's not very kind back sometimes either.

A girl in year 12 killed herself last year. That was really horrible. I didn't know her to talk to, but she always looked happy and was really, really popular. Em said she had cuts on her arms, but I never saw them.

17th February

The number of people in Italy that are dying of Coronavirus is getting higher. Em and her family were supposed to be going there this week for half term, but they've cancelled their holiday. It's such a shame - she's really miserable about it. They might have to cancel the school trip there as well if it carries on.

19th February

OMG .. seriously .. there was a totally ridiculous conversation in the family WhatsApp today. Grandpa ended up leaving the group - he keeps doing that every time someone irritates him. Then Auntie Sophie has to let him join again.

The Brit awards was on last night - Ella and Grandpa had a MASSIVE row about it … and then everyone else joined in ..

Ella: It was a well brilliant show ..
Grandpa: Stop talking rubbish. Who were they?? I didn't know who any of them were apart from Ronnie Wood and Rod Stewart. It's not MUSIC, it's a bloody nonsense .. it was just a load of NOISE. Where's the talent? I don't understand it.
Auntie Sophie: Why on earth were you watching it Dad? It's not your sort of thing.
Auntie Ellie: I thought it was powerful political commentary .. shining a light on deep endemic racism and blatant media bias.
Ella : Wot? I literally don't know wot you are on about Auntie. Like EVER?
Auntie Ellie: Frankly I despair …
Neville: I liked the Bond Theme - I thought that was alright as it goes.
Me: Billie Eilish is the best.
Grandma: Which one was he?
Ella: He's not a he !!
Grandma: Oh is he not?? What is he then ? … is he one of these new people that are a bit of both? "Thems" or whatever they are called?
Ella: Grandma … seriously I can't even.
Grandma: Those other boys were very handsome. I liked Dave and that Stormy chap looked like he was having a lovely time.
Grandpa: Dave? Dave? What kind of name is that for a rock musician?
Ella: Seriously Grandpa? What are you on about rock for ? That's not a thing … cos it's like Grime yeah?
Grandpa: What's like grime?
Ella : Forget it Grandpa. Dave's like totally Sic. Anyway I thought it was well good … apart from those weird old blokes at the end. That was well boring, and they was proper sad - wot was going on with their hair ?

** Jack Brady left the group **

22nd February

We went to London today to see the Musical Six - it was soooooo good. Really brilliant dancing and singing and really funny. I LOVE musicals. We are going to "Everyone's talking about Jamie" later in the year.

Lots of people are coming back from holidays in Italy and they are all worried about the Coronavirus. Em said she's really glad they didn't go on their holiday now. It was probably a good idea - at least they will be safe now.

23rd February

OMG. NIGHTMARE of a Sunday lunch at Grandma and Grandpas....
Grandma was annoyed because she'd made a really lovely roast leg of lamb with ALL the trimmings and Mum wouldn't touch it. She brought her own nut roast (which looked REVOLTING) and kept going on about animal carcasses!

Seriously ... disgusting.

Grandpa was still angry with Ella after the Brit Awards argument on WhatsApp. He just kept saying, "I just can't believe you don't know who Rod and Ronnie are??? I mean they are LEGENDS."

Ella said, "Well, I just don't Grandpa .. like I said they are well old. I never even heard any music they done."

So Grandpa said they are on the radio ALL the time and she said the radio is just for Boomers and everyone else listens to Spotify.

Then Grandpa said, "Well it's a bloody nonsense. You know who Freddy Mercury is ..... and Elton John. I know you do. I've heard you talk about them."

Ella replied, "Yeah .. well that's 'cos they've both got films yeah? And that Elton John yeah? He done the John Lewis Christmas Ad as well. So he's like .. proper famous. But those other blokes .. they haven't got films have they?"

Grandpa went to get another beer so he didn't have to keep talking to her. Then Auntie Ellie facetimed and said she was just saying hello quickly and didn't have time to chat because she was off to take part in a LGBTQIAPK demonstration.

Grandpa got even more annoyed and said, "What a load of rubbish. It used to be LGBT - I understood what that meant. What are all these other letters? Are they just making stuff up?"

Neville chimed in and said, "If they carry on adding letters on I'm going to need a Sesame Street style song to be able to remember them all."And Ella said, "Wot's Sesame Street ? Is that another crap band that Boomers like?"

Then Grandpa lost his temper and shouted, "oh for goodness stop talking bollocks" to Ella and she shouted "Ok Boomer" at him, and Grandma shouted, "don't say bollocks Jack!" and he said, "I'll say what I bloody well want to say - bloody bollocks to the lot of you."

Then Neville said .. "and today's argument is brought to you by the Letter B."

For some reason him, Mum, Uncle Dave and Auntie Sally thought that was really funny, but me and Ella didn't get it.

Later on Grandma put a comment in the family WhatsApp saying she thought Grandpa was developing some sort of pensioner's Tourettes.

25th February

It's Pancake Day. I love pancake day. Mum is supposed to be off refined sugar, but started rattling on about Mercury retrograde playing havoc with her creativity and saying that all the unpredictable energetic vibrations around her need to be comforted with sugary food. She said "It's so important that I listen to my body" and took me into town for a fancy strawberry and Nutella pancake. It was actually quite nice to spend time with her - even if she's being weird about "energetic forces" all the time. But then she took a picture of her Vegan blueberry pancake and said, "that'll be perfect for The Gram" and ruined the whole thing.

Neville's been trying to be funny. He's been making "tosser" jokes all day. We are both ignoring him, so he just keeps repeating the same jokes for us. Same as last year and every other pancake day I can remember !

I found a hilarious YouTube clip where someone had put a pancake over a dog's face. So funny. That pissed him off a bit. He muttered something about me and Mum having no sense of humour.

Since we'd already had pancakes in town he just made one for himself. I said, "Who looks a right tosser now then?" which made him mis-flip his pancake and drop it on the floor.

The dog was happy.

26th February

Mum MADE me take the dog for a walk tonight - she said I spent the whole of half term doing "absolutely nothing and monging about on the sofa." I was about to shout at her and tell her how unfair that is, but .. actually … I DID literally spend the whole week on the sofa. I put some plates in the dishwasher on Wednesday though so she can't claim I did ABSOLUTELY nothing !!

The dog is a total liability.
She pooed FOUR times.
FOUR !!
I don't know what's wrong with her. I was trying to pick one up and she got her lead wrapped around this old lady's legs and nearly pulled her over into the mud. It was a NIGHTMARE. And she was aggressive to EVERY single dog that walked past.

I am literally NEVER taking her out again.

I complained about it to Grandma .. but that was a waste of time …..

Grandma said - what do you mean you laid on the sofa all week? That's just bone idle ..
Grandpa said - when I was your age I had 3 different jobs, you young layabouts don't know you're born ..
Uncle John said - I got physically booted out the house and told to find work every school holiday ..
Mum said - Ellie and I spent our holidays looking after Uncle Dave and Auntie Sophie because Grandma worked full time ..
Auntie Sophie said - I thought you were the one that really wanted a dog Ruby?
Ellie said - you could be volunteering Ruby or donating your time to a homeless shelter ..
Neville said - blimey .. and I thought I was a lazy sod ..
Ella said - ignore all the Boomers Ruby, school is like well stressful .. adults don't get how it's like … loads of pressure yeah? …

I told Mum I saw Debbie when I was out - her whole family are walking round in face masks 'cos of the Coronavirus. Even the dog's got one on.

29th February

Someone died of the Coronavirus in England today - the papers are saying there might be loads more - like in Italy.

3rd March

Neville is getting pretty worked up about this virus. He's on his phone ALL the time reading stuff on Twitter and looking at news sites. He keeps saying we are just not taking it seriously enough.

He's changed his tune. Two weeks ago he was saying that any virus named after a beer can't be a bad thing.

Mum isn't really worried and just keeps saying it will work out as it's supposed to - not very helpful.

He just shouted, "That's rubbish Jaz … other countries are shutting down completely, they are closing the borders, everyone's wearing masks and we are just being told to wash our hands and sing happy birthday twice. Boris is even going round announcing that he's been in hospitals shaking hands with Coronavirus patients. This is not going to end well, you mark my words."

6th March

Everything's going a bit mad with the Coronavirus. Boris went on This Morning and said that perhaps people could "take it on the chin" and "let it move through the population." That doesn't sound helpful. Other countries are completely closing. I'm a bit confused. He also said that we've got a fantastic NHS .. which is true.

People that have symptoms - like a cough or temperature - are supposed to self isolate now.

Also they are saying they might shut school for 2 WEEKS (which would be BRILLIANT). Not so brilliant is the fact people are panic-buying stuff in the supermarkets - there's no pasta or bleach or toilet rolls in some of the shops! You can't get hand sanitiser and soap either. Grandpa says it's bloody ridiculous and keeps asking if no-one was washing their hands or cleaning their houses before this all happened.

In China people are wearing big plastic water bottles on their heads so they don't catch anything .. it's mad.

Everyone's using the word "scaremongering" again.

That's annoying. That's what people did all the time when Brexit was going on.

Mum is in a bad mood with Neville - he went to the pub yesterday after work "for one drink" with work people and ended up staying all night. He sent a text saying he was self-isolating in the pub, because the barman had just sneezed over the 4 packets of crisps that Fat Pam bought, and he wanted to protect us! Mum rang him immediately to say he should come home and do something useful and that he shouldn't call her Fat Pam. He ignored that, he was too busy ranting about the fact she'd already had a burger and chips, but she still ate all 4 bags herself and spent the next 10 minutes working out all the syns on her Slimming World App.

9th March

Mum is properly off on one today … she woke me up at 5am banging around the house going on about absorbing the energy of the new Super Moon. She keeps saying 2020 started with incredible potent cosmic energy ..

Now she's collecting a whole load of stuff for some kind of moon ritual .. she has rice and petals, lots of candles and one of her t-shirts. She said she has to write down things to release, then drop the rice and the petals while chanting stuff, then everything has to be bundled up in the t-shirt and held over the biggest candle.

Honestly. Where does she find this stuff ?? I said I thought it was a waste of a good t-shirt, but she said it was Virgo Moon Ritual and "we heal through release and acceptance as we move forward.."

Neville said, “what the hell are you on about now Jaz? Dropping bits of rice on an old t-shirt ffs.”

So she gave him one of her looks (like she thinks he’s a complete idiot) and said, “Neville the current energy is accelerating spiritual growth and means that we are all ascending into higher levels of consciousness … it’s a beautiful time for the planet.”

He replied, “a beautiful time for the planet??? Are you off your actual nut??? So far this year there’s floods everywhere, fires have been destroying Australia, Coronavirus is sweeping the planet and there are ACTUAL PLAGUES of massive locusts in Africa .. This is LITERALLY how the world is supposed to end … and I’m stuck in this f’ing house with a bloody moon-worshiping lunatic and limited bog roll !! If ever there was a time to go to the Winchester for a pint and wait for it all to blow over it’s NOW.”

** PS: Neville’s been on about the Winchester for years … I finally saw Sean of the Dead, so I understand him at last !

** PPS: Grandpa rang to say when he was little they had to cut up bits of newspaper to use for toilet paper and everyone’s making a fuss about nothing. He sounded quite cheerful .. I think he’s hoping he gets to do it again.

10th March

It’s Mum’s Birthday today - normally she does something with the girls or goes out for dinner with Neville, but she’s in a really weird mood - she didn’t really want to do anything .. she’s been wandering around looking tearful and saying she’s now got a really bad feeling about this whole virus and everything feels “heavy.”

She’d booked a meditation & healing workshop in Glastonbury this coming weekend, but she’s now cancelled it and says she’s “listening to her intuition.” She went for a run this morning, but went on her own instead of with the group she joined. They’ve ended up breaking into smaller groups, because they can’t run near each other and chat like normal, so she said she'd spend some time "with herself."

It's saying on the news that people with ANY symptoms like a cough or especially a temperature shouldn't leave their houses!

Mum opened her presents and had a glass of Prosecco - then she went for a long bath and went to bed without saying goodnight to anyone. I hope she isn't going to get weird again like last year … she used to spend hours in bed staring at the wall.

Neville suggested me and him watch Contagion on Netflix. He said "It's about a deadly virus that causes a global pandemic killing millions of people. This leads to the total breakdown of society, whilst they desperately search for a vaccine."

I said it sounded a bit unrealistic and he should just watch it on his own.

11th March

Mum was still in bed when I went to school. When I got home she was out. It turned out she'd taken the dog for a long walk. It was obvious she'd been crying. When I asked her what was wrong she said she'd been watching all the little kids playing in the park after school and it had made her really, really sad.

She said, "the sun was shining and they were all running around laughing and squealing and it just feels like the end of normal life. I have this huge weight in the centre of my chest - I feel like something terrible is about to happen."

Later on she sent Neville to the shops to buy a load of stuff to make healthy food to boost our immune systems. She said, "just get what you can Neville, you might struggle to find any of it .. people are going completely mad in the shops."

He said, "I think we will be good Jaz, I'm pretty sure no one is panic buying fennel seeds and cumin."

12th March

Mum has left the cafe as it's takeaway only now and they don't need many staff. They think they will have to completely shut pretty soon anyway as that's what happened in Spain and Italy. They keep saying they didn't close the pubs, and restaurants and cafes fast enough over there and that is why things got really bad because everyone was still mixing in groups and hugging each other. Everyone here is still being told to carry on and wash their hands. But some people are leaving offices and starting to work from home if they can do that.

Mum said Ollie is really upset about the cafe. I'm not surprised - it was going really well and he was just about to open his next cafe and now he can't .. and he will probably have to shut this one. I know Neville doesn't like him, but I think he has lots of great ideas and he works really hard.

Neville is still going into his office at the moment, but he's going to be working at home soon.

13th March

Today turned out to be my last day at school for a while - Mum said she's not listening to the Government anymore. She's "taking matters into her own hands," because they should have shut the schools already. She said she won't be sending me back in on Monday. I don't mind - I'm quite happy not to go to school. I can talk to my friends from home.

Mary came over this evening .. She's had her hair braided and dyed purple - that's new. She's pretty annoying .. she's always rattling on about crystals and the importance of honouring everyone's spiritual aura. OMG they have the MOST ridiculous conversations ..

seriously, they were talking about the Coronavirus and saying it's important to stay in a vibrational frequency that doesn't allow illness to reach you. Mary kept wafting her sage stick around every single time Neville came in the room and muttering about stale energy and moon cycles.

Neville's not happy either. He said they'll probably need to cancel Chemical Banana's gig next week . He said it's looking inevitable, because there's talk of the Government enforcing the cancellation of ALL large gatherings of people.

I actually spat out my hot chocolate laughing when he said that .. LARGE gatherings??? Seriously??? .... Chemical Banana have NEVER had more than about 9 people in the room at any of their gigs (and that includes the actual band!).

Later on Mum showed me this video that was making fun of spiritual people … she said, "It's such an exaggeration - it's so funny!" Exaggeration?? It was stupidly dressed people sitting around saying stuff like "I totally honour your opinion" and "I'm holding space for you and your aura." Her and Mary thought it was hilarious - but that is LITERALLY what the two of them sound like.

When it was time for Mary to leave they both had a really dramatic hug and said they shouldn't get together anymore as everyone is supposed to be staying home and not touching each other - Mary said, "We must stay positive and in a high vibration to honour this important planetary shift."

Honestly … what nonsense.

The adults do all seem a bit worried … it's making me a bit scared … although on the internet it says that kids don't catch it .. only old people. But that just made me scared for Grandpa and Grandma and Neville's Dad.

14th March

DAY 1 OF STAYING AT HOME - Mum's pretending to be relaxed and going on about the change in consciousness being "positive," but at the same time she's really worked up. I can tell because she's just told Neville to go and buy loads of wine.

15th March

Everything is really strange .. the TV channels and the papers are full of bad news and talking about the numbers of people dying in Italy. There are also videos of people stuck in flats and singing to each other from their balconies - that bit is quite nice, but it must be horrid. They aren't allowed out except for food and medicine and the police are on the streets checking everyone's paperwork. It's REALLY, REALLY strict.

16th March

It's Monday, and Mum has stuck to her word for once and isn't letting me go to school today because it's too dangerous. She said she thinks the Government is moving much too slowly. Neville keeps saying "The writing was on the wall weeks ago with Spain and Italy, but Boris ignored it." Mum said she thinks our school should be closed already - businesses are now preparing to shut, so the schools won't be far behind. I don't mind, I'm happy at home. She said they will probably have to shut in a few days anyway.

Mum tried to get some more toilet rolls today, but the shelves were totally empty. Completely mad. I feel sorry for the staff in Tescos - Mum said some people are being really rude to them. It's not their fault. There was no soap anywhere either .. luckily we still have some of both because Mum always has a bit of a "stash" as she calls it. Neville had to buy hand sanitiser for work, the corner shop was charging £9.99 for a tiny bottle. He WASN'T happy.

Mum is doing loads more meditating and FaceTiming people - whenever I walk past she's saying stupid things about the consciousness of the planet and how the role of sacred sisterhood has never been more important. I'm trying to take no notice. Mum was planning to visit Grandma's house today for a cup of tea, but decided it wasn't a good idea as Grandma and Grandpa are over 70 and they are supposed to be staying in and not mixing with anyone - just to be safe. She was really sad about it.

Boris did a press conference thing on TV and everyone is talking about "flattening the curve." I don't really get it, but it's something to do with not too many people needing to be in the hospital at the same time.

17th March

The Coronavirus stuff is getting pretty weird and scary now. Everywhere's a LOT quieter than usual.

Em and Charlotte are still at school - they said that the teachers told the whole school that anyone who coughs has to go home immediately. 60 kids got sent home today!!! Neville said, "well if you tell a bunch of teenagers that they'll be able to go home if they cough, stands to reason the whole lot will start coughing - little buggers. What did the school think would happen, FFS?"

Mum says there is something called 'Full Lockdown' happening really soon, where there are really strict rules like in all the other countries and we will all have to stay in our houses for a really, really long time. Everyone is going crazy stockpiling and Boris is suddenly looking very serious on TV.

Every time Neville gets home he says some version of a sentence involving the words "people", "f***ing" and "bog rolls."

He just came back moaning about what he couldn't find - he said there are just totally empty shelves in some bits of the shop. He even took a photo to prove it to us.

There was no:

Toilet Rolls, Kitchen Rolls or tissues
Liquid soap or hard soap
Antibac wipes or any kind of wipes (even for babies)
Hand sanitiser
Flash, Dettol, Bleach, Cillit Bang or anything for cleaning
Pasta .. even the gluten free stuff (Mum said that's not fair for the celiac people that can't eat the other stuff)
Pot noodles
Flour for making bread
Boxes of Hair Dye

The hair dye is annoying, I've decided to dye my hair dark, just for a change really. But it seems like everyone else must be thinking the same thing and buying the boxed stuff because all the hairdressers will be closing soon. Mind you I couldn't really trust Neville to get the right thing. Mum's managed to order one online, but it doesn't say how long it will take - all their stock is out too.

Panic-buying is happening everywhere in the world - people are just stockpiling different things, Americans are queuing to buy more guns, people in Holland are queuing outside the special coffee shops and in England we are fighting over toilet rolls.

Tonight Neville said, "So this is how it all ends .. the Yanks are going to be shooting more people, the Dutch will all be stoned out of their skulls, and as for us lot, apparently, we are all gonna be sh*tting ourselves."

Then he added, "Tell you something though Jaz - the f***ing vegans will survive The Apocalypse .. there was barely an item missing on those shelves and I went to 4 different shops this evening."

18th March

Mum is all about "raising our vibrational energy" and "staying grounded" so we don't get pulled into "the mass hysteria and the fear consciousness that is sweeping the planet."

Auntie Ellie is sharing lots of helpful science articles on the family WhatsApp and everyone else is trying to keep cheerful posting lots of jokes and memes. Grandma has even worked out how to forward funny TikTok videos. If nothing else they are getting better with technology during all this.

Neville spends most of his time on Twitter constantly announcing various death statistics from different countries and googling articles about conspiracy theories.

He walked in the kitchen holding his phone and said, "Listen to this Jaz, Donald Trump just said, "people are dying who have never died before." That's helpful isn't it? Covid can't kill you more than once. Cheers Donald .. sound advice."

Mum told him it sounded like Fake News as even Trump can't be THAT stupid, and that you shouldn't believe anything you see on the internet. She also told him she didn't want to hear any more details because she was protecting her energy by not focusing on the virus. Then she started to burn a smudge stick and waft it all over the lounge .. I went to my room because I hate the smell, but it made Neville start choking and I heard him shouting,"cut it out Jaz you know I've got asthma FFS."

School is closing for good on Friday - all the other countries have shut their schools already and the government is now admitting that's the next inevitable step.

OMG - the GCSEs and the A' levels have been cancelled !! The year 11s are sooooooooo lucky … I mean I know it's terrible because of all the people that are dying, but NO EXAMS ? Seriously … SO jealous.

19th March

Loads of Mums clients have cancelled as they are all worried about their jobs and don't want to pay for stuff - she can do some of her work online, but she's still had all her big projects cancelled or postponed. Neville is still going into work. He has been arguing with Keith Kitchen about the fact that he should be working at home as he's an "at risk" employee due to his asthma.

Auntie Sophie, Uncle Marc and Uncle Dave are all working at home now. Auntie Sally has gone to London to get her Mum so she can stay with them and Ella is packing up her Uni stuff because they are collecting her tomorrow and bringing her home.

When Neville got home, there was a serious talk about money going on in the kitchen, he should still get paid, as his job is something to do with getting essential food supplies to shops, but they are worried as Mum is self-employed and she doesn't have hardly any money coming in.

Neville will be working at home from Monday. Keith Kitchen insisted on asking for a medical certificate and checking with HR before he signed it off. He's not happy. He just said, "that idiot sees me with my inhaler every day .. does he think I'm doing it for fun??"

Everywhere is definitely much quieter when you go out. There aren't very many cars and hardly anyone wandering around like normally. I only went to the little Tesco so it might be different in other places. It's really strange and a bit scary seeing people queuing with masks on and these big spaces between each other. Everyone is either completely silent or talking really quietly. Neville keeps calling it "The Apocalypse."

Yesterday he said, "I really thought when The Apocalypse happened there'd be more Zombies and fewer conversations about toilet paper …"

20th March - DAY 7 at home

It's Friday and school officially closed today - not that there were many people left there anyway. We are all going to be studying at home.

It's strange us all being at home, I think it's quite nice. I've been sleeping in pretty late and wearing my PJs around the house. Mum's been drinking every night and doing the same thing. Apart from the mornings when she gets up at 5 and wanders around the fields. She said she can't sleep properly and is having really weird dreams ….

The pubs also have to close completely tonight. Neville insisted on going out for one more pint. Him and Mum had an absolutely massive row about it. Mum said, "It's irresponsible Neville, I think you should stay here. They are closing because it's dangerous to be in enclosed places next to lots of other people. It's not an invitation to rush out for one last germ-fest." He went anyway, but said he'd stand on his own and not talk to anyone.

He said, "Stop going on about it Jaz, it's all bloody exaggerated, and anyway it won't be a problem if the usual suspects are there - I don't like any of those twats anyway - I never talk to them on a normal night."

Mum told him if he goes to the pub he will have to self-isolate in the spare room for the next 2 weeks. He went anyway.

21st March

Neville spent the whole day ranting about the fact that there are so many people out and about. The news is terrible - people are supposed to be staying in, but there are people having picnics in parks in London and a huge queue of cars going up to Snowdon.

He was shouting, "What's wrong with people??? Don't they get it?? This isn't the time to be going out enjoying yourself - this is serious. Didn't they listen to the news yesterday? "

So Mum said, "That's rich coming from the idiot that spent the whole of last night in a packed pub!"

He shouted, "That's different - I was supporting a local business - people's livelihoods are at stake here Jaz."

Me, Em and Alice went to hang out in the park for a bit. Probably the last time we get to do that for a while. I think it's OK as kids aren't even getting this anyway.

It might be really busy in London and up Snowdon, but it's not busy round here. It's actually really quiet and eerie everywhere - there aren't any kids playing on the swings today. I said that to Mum and she said that it was seeing the kids playing in the park last week that kept making her cry.

It's really strange … it kind of feels like there is a sense of doom hanging over the world …..

22nd March

Today is Mother's Day. With all the weirdness going on I totally forgot about it and I didn't get a present or card or anything. Neville said he'd make a nice dinner so I got him to get some wine for her and something nice for pudding.

Mum had bought these really fancy iced biscuits to give to Grandma, but she wasn't really supposed to go and see her so she sent her a photo of them instead. I asked if Mum could just have them as a gift from me since I'd forgotten .. so she did that. I helped her eat them though.

There were some pictures of people on social media sitting in their Mum's gardens with a big space between them having a class of fizz. There's an Old lady over the road called Mrs Wilson, who just became a grandma for the first time. I saw her meeting her little granddaughter through the front window. She couldn't even hold her. How sad is that ?

Mrs Wilson has a heart condition and is having to stay inside. It's called "shielding." All old people and vulnerable people with illnesses are having to do it. Mrs Wilson's family don't live nearby, so when we properly lock down they won't be able to visit her. I think that's why her daughter brought the baby round today.

That made me cry properly for the first time. Mum said it was breaking her heart and went out for a long walk on her own with her earphones in.

Monday 23rd March - OFFICIAL LOCKDOWN DAY 1 (10 days at home for us)

Boris made a really important speech on the TV and we all sat and watched it together.

Grandma got all nostalgic on the WhatApp and said, "It must have been like this in the war when people sat listening to announcements on their radios .. mind you they called it the wireless back then." And Ella said, "Seriously Grandma? I thought all the wireless stuff was well modern." I think Grandpa was going to try and explain as the 3 dots kept coming up and going away and it said *Jack Brady is typing* … then it stopped again and he disappeared completely.

The government has made a special slogan.

They like slogans. It's like when they kept saying "Strong and Stable" and "Brexit means Brexit."

This one is "Stay at Home - Protect the NHS - Save Lives." Boris was trying to look all serious and said something like if you can work at home, work at home, and if you can't work at home go to work, but try not to go to work and don't go on public transport, unless you have to, in which case go on public transport ….

Mum said essentially it means that everyone should work at home if they can and "non-essential" businesses should shut completely .. so stuff like bars, pubs, restaurants, cinemas, nightclubs, theatres, gyms and leisure centres and churches.

People that have to go to work like nurses and shop workers and stuff are being called "Key Workers," now. They still have to go out and carry on even if they are scared about catching the virus. There are some teachers that are staying at school to look after the key worker's kids. All the other kids have to be homeschooled.

We knew this was coming because all the other countries have done it, so it wasn't really that big a deal. It's not even as strict really because we can exercise and we don't have the police watching everyone like in Spain and Italy. Everyone is allowed to go out and exercise once a day. Only "essential" shops like food shops and the Chemists - or the Pharmacy as Uncle John calls it - can stay open.

We FaceTimed Uncle John to see how they are getting on. He said everything is fine in America - it doesn't look like that on the news though .... We thought everything was fine here when things were bad in Italy and now everyone is actually getting worried because the number of deaths is going up really fast. I expect that will happen in America too. All the individual states are doing different things, Mum's friend in California says that they locked down early, but stuff is still open where Uncle John lives.

Emmy-Lou wasn't there when we called. Uncle John said she'd just popped out to Walmart to get another gun.

He said, "What's the story over there with all the toilet paper stockpiling?" Neville said, "No idea mate, just people behaving like idiots really." So John said, "there's a bit of that going on here as well - I don't get it, you can pretty much use anything to wipe your bum really can't you?" Then he told a story about when he was younger and he used to help his milkman mate out sometimes, they had to get up really early to deliver the milk and he often got caught out needing the loo on the way round. He said, "yeah, I remember it well ... many's the time I had to wipe my arse on the special-offer cheese vouchers..."

26th March - LOCKDOWN day 4

Well .. I haven't written anything much for a few days because it's all just been really weird !

All the schools officially closed on Friday (not that there were many people left) and that's it now for the rest of the year.The year 6's didn't get any leaving parties and the year 11's didn't get a prom. They don't have to do any exams which is brilliant for them but it's such a sad end to school really.

Everywhere is pretty much closed now. Mum said the only people out today were a few old people queuing outside the Chemist and the scruffy bloke that drinks beer out of a paper bag at the bus stop. Oh and a few teenagers hanging about.

People are going out for their daily "Boris Walk" as Mum calls it. The Appleby's are all going out on a family bike ride everyday - they come past our house sometimes, all in a row, looking pretty unhappy. You can hear Terence saying stuff like, "Keep it moving Martha, our pace has just slowed, stop letting the side down for goodness sake." She texted Mum after to say how much she hates cycling and that she's sick of pretending to be enjoying herself.

Her facebook still looks like everything's perfect mind you. She's posting the kids' photo lockdown diary every day. There's cakes and craft projects and what looks like a very busy timetable on the kitchen wall.

Me and Mum take the dog out most evenings .. it's very peaceful. Everyone kind of walks around quietly like someone is having a nap and you are trying not to disturb them. Most people make space on the paths for each other and say "good evening" most of the time - some people push past you like they don't know what social distancing is. Sometimes Neville comes with us, but most of the time he goes out on his own with his earphones in and listens to podcasts. He says he prefers that. I actually like it when it's just me and Mum. Sometimes we talk, but often it's just a quiet walk … which is nice.

There's hardly any traffic in town really which is very strange and you can't really hear anything on the motorway - which we used to when things were normal. You only see delivery vans from food shops and a few cars. Occasionally a bus goes past with no-one on it. Sometimes we see people park on the street and put on a load of protective plastic and masks and go into the house where Mr Marshall lives on his own. He's very old. I hope he's OK.

The neighbours have set up a WhatsApp group for the road in case people have to isolate and also if they need someone to shop for them or help out - it's mostly for the old people like Mrs Wilson and Mr Marshall - especially if they are on their own. I think it's nice, but Neville is getting annoyed because Derek and Doreen from No.16 are on there all the time going on about rules and talking about how fabulous Boris is all the time. Mum and Neville think he's messing everything up because he didn't lockdown quickly and the airports are all still open and there's no testing, so they just don't comment.

Mum asked Mr Marshall if he needed any essential food items last week because she was going shopping and he asked for a loaf of bread, a jar of pickled onions and 2 bottles of Whiskey. Mum said, what about some bacon or some meat ? He said no, then he said, "I tell you what Janice, get me a couple of tins of tuna fish." That made Mum feel a bit better about him getting at least a bit of nutrition, but it turned out that was for the cat. I didn't think it sounded very healthy at all, but Neville said, "It's that generation, my Grandma lasted years on nothing but Weetabix, Brown Ale and cigarettes.

Everyone is online ALL DAY, so the wifi is rubbish. Mum is trying to get me to do Joe Wicks workouts at 9 o'clock in the morning and I'm so bored that I've finally managed to dye my hair for something to do. Mum managed to find some dye in Tesco because they restocked. The online one hasn't come yet.

It's really dark which actually looks great - I think I did a great job - Mum says it's easy to have disasters when you try and do your own hair. Everyone will be doing that for a while though as they can't go to the actual hairdressers..

Speaking of hair Dan, Connor, James 1 & 2 and Jake have all shaved their heads because we aren't in school. Jake's really suits him, because he's pretty gorgeous. But the others look terrible. Dan has a really funny-shaped head ….. you couldn't tell before.

We haven't EVEN been in lockdown for hardly any time and I'm already fed up with people talking about Covid-19. We are all supposed to be protecting the vulnerable people and only going out if we really have to. It feels really quiet around here, but the newspapers are full of tons of people packed onto tube trains and buses in London.

All the Mums and some Dads are homeschooling. Coco and Felix's schedule is unbelievable .. so much stuff on it, Auntie Sophie has thought of everything .. Mum said she got exhausted just reading through it and needed a sit down after.

Mum and Neville have been pretty calm about everything so far, except when Mum couldn't visit Grandma on Mother's Day and she cried. So I'm trying not to worry too much. At least we just have to stay home and not work at a hospital or anything dangerous like that.

Mum's WhatApp is pinging ALL DAY.

It's not even been a whole week of homeschool and most of her friends are starting to drink wine EVEN EARLIER in the day and moaning about the fact that wine is being rationed to 2 bottles at a time in the supermarket - honestly. Ever since the pubs shut people don't care about hoarding toilet paper anymore - they just want to hoard wine. Mind you Neville is working from home now so if Mum runs out of wine I think they might ACTUALLY kill each other.

Off Licences and DIY/Hardware stores have been added to the list of places that can stay open. Grandma says it's typical of this country that shops selling alcohol are considered "Essential."

Neville working from home is actually really annoying. He's walking round the house with EarPods in trying to sound important .. he keeps saying things like, "we need to reach some alignment," "lets circle back," "we should really drill this down," and "I simply don't have the bandwidth right now Keith." That's annoying.

He's such an idiot.

And he's doing conference calls in his pants.

Mum was all excited about homeschooling, because she was a teacher for a bit, years and years ago. She keeps saying that she can help to teach me.

OMG. I can only imagine!

I told her I don't need her to do anything, because it's all on Google Classroom, but the younger kids have all got their parents helping them - poor them is all I can say. About the only thing Mum's friends would be good at, is teaching their kids how to open bottles of wine!!

She did try to make me help her make some soup earlier saying it was "Food Tech." I'm not even doing Food Tech. But I quite like cooking so I didn't moan at her. I like soup, and also she keeps going on about me keeping my immune system healthy, which does seem like a good idea.

Mum's friend Jane just sent a WhatsApp saying she was helping her little 7 year old daughter with some maths and hadn't noticed the pen she was using .. The pen says "Don't touch my f***ing pen" - honestly none of them should be in charge of teaching kids ANYTHING ! She said her daughter is Dyslexic, so she probably didn't realise.

I'd done all my school work for today, so I spent the whole afternoon on the sofa watching Netflix. Mum tried to nag me about it, but I told her I was actually doing "Film Studies" and that she was interfering in my education.

27th March - Lockdown Day 5

Today over 900 people died in Italy in one day ! Also Boris has got the Coronavirus !! He said he's only got mild symptoms so he is just going to self-isolate and do announcements on video and not go into Parliament. Neville says it's pretty easy to social distance in Parliament since "hardly any of the lazy buggers even bother to turn up most days."

Poor Boris - I felt a bit bad for him, but Neville said, "Stupid git .. it's his own fault for going around shaking everyone's hand in the hospital and showing off about it." I said that wasn't very nice and he should be more sympathetic as it's a really scary, horrible illness. He walked off muttering something that sounded like "Bellend."

Mum says EVERYONE is working out how to put their businesses online because they can't work like they normally do. Exercise classes are going online and estate agents are doing virtual tours. All the local salons and cafes are setting up online shops so they can deliver stuff and the restaurants are doing take-away now they are shut. EVERYONE is going on about Zoom all the time and people are trying to "pivot" I don't know what that is .. the only time I've heard that is on the episode of Friends when Ross gets the sofa stuck on the stairs and just keeps shouting "PIVOT" really loudly.

Mum keeps asking Neville what she can do to get more online and remote work .. I don't get it .... she worked at home before and did everything by phone and email anyway. I don't see why she needs to do anything differently. Neville said EXACTLY the same thing. She just can't work at the cafe for now.

Speaking of the cafe - I think her "pivot" obsession is because of Ollie. He's set up a dinner delivery service for the cafe and a YouTube Channel where he does high intensity workouts and vegan cooking for fitness - all within like ONE WEEK! The channel it's gone a bit crazy in the first few days and he's getting loads of followers. It's all training for vegans (including Marathons, Triathlons and Ironman preparation). It really annoys Neville that he's done all of those. He keeps going on about something called

"Beast Mode" whatever that is .. and then saying "Beast Mode doesn't have to mean eating actual beasts remember .. protect animals, eat plants instead." Then he ends every video saying "Save the Planet. Eat Plants. Peace Out."
Neville just glanced at the screen while I was watching and said, "what an ABSOLUTE nob that bloke is."

So last night we did this thing called "Clap for Carers" it's going to be every Thursday at 8pm. We all stood on the doorstep and clapped for the NHS - it was really nice - the whole street came out. Even Derek and Doreen, who are always miserable and arguing, looked reasonably happy. There's hardly any traffic now so you could hear the sound of clapping all across town. Someone up the road was banging some saucepan lids together. The dog wasn't impressed and just went upstairs to sulk under the bed.

Mum got a bit emotional about it all.

Then she went into a big ramble afterwards about all the good that will come out of this pandemic. She said this is ALL happening because "Mother Nature has been screaming at us about climate change, but we weren't listening so the earth had to intervene. So we are now experiencing a mass cleansing of the earth itself and the whole of the global human consciousness."

But Neville said, "FFS Jaz this is all happening because some twat in China ate a f***ing BAT !! "

28th March - Lockdown Day 6

Mum and Neville are complaining about all the emails they are getting. Neville said, "seriously Jaz I haven't shopped at some of these places for about 4 years and they are suddenly contacting me to check that I'm coping in "these strange times." Honestly, even if I wasn't coping .. those people I got the lawnmower from would be the last people I'd talk to. Even the people we got the shed from have been in touch to tell me about the changes they've made relating to Covid. I really couldn't give a toss."

Mum said, "it's good customer service Neville, that's all." He replied, "it would have been better customer service to have thanked me for spending all that money on the f***ing shed, but they never did that did they."

Neville has been trying to get someone at the care home where his dad stays to help him set up a FaceTime - he's not allowed to go and visit his Dad which is really sad. The care homes have tons of people with Covid and because they are all old they are suffering really badly. Neville said young people have probably got it, but lots of them don't even have symptoms which is why they have to stay away from the old people in case they infect them and don't realise.

There's a really sweet girl there that managed to sort it out, and his Dad appeared on the screen looking a bit confused. Neville asked him how he was doing and he didn't say anything, so I popped my head over his shoulder and gave him a wave and he said "Hello Ruby," which was sweet. But it ended up being a bit sad for Neville because then he said, "Is that bloke bothering you love?" Neville got me to do most of the talking and then we said goodbye.

I heard him say, "Maybe his dementia is a blessing Jaz, he probably doesn't really know what's going on with all this Covid nonsense." Then he went and shot people on his Xbox for about 2 hours.

March 30th - Lockdown Day 8

Feels like we've been stuck at home FOREVER - but it's only been 2 and a bit weeks since I stopped going to school. They are doing a briefing on TV to tell us what is happening - this is usually someone standing behind a podium with slogans on it talking about rules that are confusing and telling us to use our common sense and keep washing our hands. That hasn't really worked so far as every day the numbers get higher and higher. But the numbers are confusing too and Mum and Neville keep saying there are different ways of working it out. Lots of the people have got other illnesses too, which makes it harder for them to survive. That's really sad.

Now BOTH Boris and Prince Charles have both got Coronavirus. So has the man who is the Chief Medical Advisor - that can't be good … and someone called Dominic Cummings who apparently helps Boris decide stuff. I don't suppose he's very important .. but it's still a shame he has it.

The shops are still missing stuff because of the panic buying idiots, so we've been eating vegetarian meals made out of stuff from tins that look like dog food and Mum spent 2 hours trying to explain to Grandma how to set up House Party. Even after that you could literally only see the tops of her and Grandpa's heads on the screen.

Sometimes the doorbell will ring and there won't be anyone there … just a little gift of some cakes or a bottle of wine. People are leaving things as surprises for each other which is really cute. Mum got some brownies from the cafe yesterday - they got left on the doorstep and someone had drawn a smiley face and written "Stay Safe" on the box.

All of us being here at the same time is a COMPLETE NIGHTMARE - Mum is in the lounge, I'm in the kitchen and Neville has taken over the spare room as his office because he came home with 2 massive computer monitors. The dog keeps going upstairs and jumping in his lap when he's talking to people on Zoom - then climbing up on the desk and blocking the whole screen. He keeps booting her out and sending her back downstairs. All his work colleagues think she's great.

When he's not upstairs he is walking around shouting all the time and doing endless video chats. Every now and again you know he's finished a conference call because he shouts stuff like "you're a f***ing nob Jeff" really loudly. At least I hope he's finished the call. I think he has, because he's really polite when he's talking to work people. At home he just swears ALL the time, but he sounds really sensible on his calls. To be fair though - since the new year when Mum brought in the swear jar he's waaaay better!

Today was a classic example of how annoying he can be. He was stomping around saying, "Well I'm looking at the forward achievables Keith and frankly it's going to be a challenge…. what? .. yeah, yeah … well, with respect Keith we ARE all on the same page, but being able to move the needle in this current crisis is just .. sorry what? No, I AM fleshing it out … no .. tell them there's no point reaching out to me right now .. what, ………… NO the country's at a f***king standstill what do you want me to say????? Alright, alright we'll take this offline." Then he shouted "you tosser and chucked something angrily at the wall.

Mum said his stress levels are affecting the energy in the house and he needs to ground himself. Typical thing for her to say.

Also Mum's been trying to make me and Neville help round the house. It's RIDICULOUS, he's trying to do his normal job, I'm trying to do school work and she hasn't even got much work to do. She should do the stuff round the house. No chance of that though, she's done a great big spreadsheet of household tasks for EVERYONE. I was sitting in the lounge doing my biology on my laptop and she said I needed to sort out the washing and put a load on. I just shouted, "I can't … I'm AT SCHOOL!! " Neville started laughing, but Mum looked really annoyed and went and did it herself.

She's also trying to get Neville to relax and do a bit of exercise - she was trying to make him do the Joe Wicks workout at 9 o'clock this morning, but he said, "give it a rest Janice you know that prick annoys the shit out of me." She said, "but it's all free and he's getting the country motivated to keep fit." Neville just said, "I don't give a crap haven't forgiven him for all that money you wasted on organic coconut oil. And all that crap about midget trees instead of broccoli. Lean in 15 my arse - didn't do you much good did it." Mum went off in a strop to her meditation shed.

I FaceTimed Grandma for a chat. Everyone's gone off House Party - it got too complicated so we do FaceTime and they are learning Zoom. Grandma and Grandpa are fine, they are just pottering around. At least they have one another to talk to, I feel sad for all the old people living alone that can't go out and about anywhere and haven't got anyone to talk to. Hopefully their families are FaceTiming them.

March 31st - Lockdown Day 9

Every single conversation that Mum and Neville are having at the moment is about something called furlow?!!? It doesn't matter if they are talking to each other or to official work people on the phone.

It's annoying. Neville even tried to tell me what it is. I literally don't care! Though it's apparently spelt furlough.

Turns out he'll be doing it from tomorrow. Whatever it is, it certainly seems to have made him really happy, he keeps smiling and whistling round the house. It's just WEIRD ! I'm used to him moaning, swearing and ranting all the time ... not actually being happy.

He got himself a pint of beer at 10 o'clock this morning and said, "Guess what Ruby, there'll be no more Zoom calls with that incompetent twat Keith. .. I feel a Call of Duty marathon coming on." Hopefully this means he'll stay out of my way - I'm the only one actually trying to do any work in this house right now !

Mum is going out for runs all the time - she calls them "Boris Runs" - that's annoying. She just came back with a purple face looking like she's about to have a heart attack.

And she keeps trying to help me with my school work - when she's not moaning to the "gang" about the supermarkets rationing the wine. Wouldn't do her any harm to have her wine rationed to be honest.She's already had 3 glasses this afternoon and keeps asking if I've got any MacBeth assignments to do. I don't know why she thinks she can help .. she was at school SO long ago they didn't even DO GCSEs.

Sounds like the Mums with all the little kids are getting in even more of a state - they were all trying to do English, Maths and Science lessons for about 3 days - now they are all just downloading House Party, starting on the wine earlier in the day and leaving Joe Wicks, David Walliams and Carol Vordeman to teach the kids online. Or the kids are just trashing the house or playing in the garden. That sounds way more fun than hopeless Mums pretending they know ANYTHING about teaching.

Oh God - Mum's decided we need to do home baking together as a family bonding activity ...she's found some yeast and wants to make her own bread. It's a stupid idea, there's loads of bread in the shops, this will be a total disaster.
She shared a meme,in the family WhatsApp, which said, "the real emergency will be in 20 years when these kids are adults, running the world with a home education brought to them by day drinking."

She put a bunch of crying/laughing emojis after it like it's a joke.

It's not. It's literally what her and all her friends are doing. At least I'm old enough to sort my own school work out.

1st April - Lockdown Day 10

So lockdown started quite well - it was a bit weird, all of us being home together all the time, but we got up like normal and got dressed like normal and went on our official walk every day. Like Mum actually insisted on it. EVERY DAY. It was actually quite peaceful and relaxing for a few days. Then Mum got all worked up and started banging on about rotas for cleaning and DIY and everyone doing Joe Wicks workouts, painting watercolours, and growing vegetables.

Neville forwarded a text pretending it was from the school saying that we had to go back. It was obvious it was an April fool and it wasn't even funny. I told him that and he said, "Fair point Ruby, no April fools joke would even compare with the absolute sh*t going on in the world right now."

Neville was reading a twitter thread about what your quarantine name is .. you make it up by saying how you are feeling + the last thing that you ate.

A guy called @GibranSaleem started it with "My name is sick bat" and lots of people followed with their names.

@headinmccloud - Rage Cheerios
@heidiernst - Despair Brownie
@em_i_lis - Furious Cottage Cheese
@TinaRN1120 - Drunk salami
@zakclapham - Depressed Waffle
@bullofbitcoin - Homosexual Easter Egg
@kellysmelly69 - Slovenly Bagel
@ChrisShockley76 - Irritated Whopper

My favourite was @GrahamG14843952 - who said " Fucked off mashed potato."

Mind you … not everyone got that it was a joke - in between people were saying stuff like

"Wait - what dude, you ate a bat ?"
"Did he eat a bat ?? "
"NO … he must be joking . … isn't that how this whole thing started?"

The best one was like the 10th person who said, "You ate a bat??" and he said, "Well it all depends on what was in that KFC bucket."

It thought it was obvious it was meant to be a joke, Neville agreed and said, "Honestly, looks like COVID makes some people lose their sense of smell, taste AND humour."

We worked out ours. Mine would be Bored Custard cream, Neville's would be Ranting Sausage Roll and Mum said hers would be Blissful Pinot Grigio, as she hasn't eaten for hours because she's doing "intermittent fasting." Neville told her you can't drink wine as that defeats the whole point of fasting - it's herbal tea or water only. It's not true that she's fasting anyway, I saw her stuffing a wagon wheel in her face in the garden, when she thought no-one was looking.

2nd April - Lockdown Day 11

We are officially on Day 11 of Lockdown (day 21 for me and Mum being home) and we have a bit of a routine now for each of us…..

Mum:

5am or about 10am-12am - Mum gets up.

If it's early then she'll be dressed in running gear by the time I get up and have already been out photographing the sunrise and gushing about nature on Facebook. She will then spend half the day rattling on about the sound of birdsong, seeing bees return to the garden, the beauty of the planet and the kindness of the human race. I will likely get a lecture about nature having pressed "the pause button" and how we should all be seeing the "beauty in the world and each other."

Then she will do some journaling or attempt to paint something. Then she will spend the rest of the day asking me and Neville constantly what we'd like for dinner.

If it's later that she gets up, she will mostly mope around the house in her PJs. Occasionally she'll change out of PJs into something else that looks like PJs - I can't tell the difference, but she insists they are "day clothes" if you ask her. She mostly lies on the sofa eating any combination of biscuits, cakes, bagels, haribos, or chocolate that can be found in the house. Occasionally someone will turn up on the doorstep from a local business and drop off something filled with sugar and covered in chocolate that they've lovingly made and I will have to make sure I grab some and hide it in case she eats all of it. She might go out to do essential shopping (this is usually wine or Gin) and she might occasionally do something on her laptop which usually includes shouting at Neville saying "you are on furlough it's fine for you" and "try being self employed and keeping your business afloat."

4pm - Wine usually gets opened - it's sometimes earlier, and occasionally later, it depends on whether it's a nice sunny day.

If it's earlier then things go steadily downhill with her and Neville either arguing or giggling like teenagers in the lounge. If the wine is opened later then she will normally drag us all on our allowed daily walk together beforehand and tell us that we should all be appreciating this special time together as a family and practising gratitude. Sometimes she'll do what she calls a "mental health check-in" and try and get us to sit together and talk about our feelings - so annoying.

6-7pm - Dinner - everyone pretends to be excited about dinner, but really we are all bored with ALL the meals we are having … I don't know why as we all had meals together before lockdown and it wasn't something to moan about. Although I suppose we ate out a fair bit.

8pm - about 3 nights a week Mum goes on Zoom in the kitchen with a different set of girlfriends and spends half the night getting drunk and shrieking at the computer for hours on end.

Neville:

10am - Neville gets up - most days he bounces happily round the house saying, "this not having to work business is absolutely brilliant." Occasionally he doesn't appear until mid-afternoon and when that happens, he just looks angry and walks around muttering "what's the f'ing point?"

11am - takes the dog for a long walk.

12am - has a lunchtime beer.

1pm - goes to play on the xbox.

3pm - completely ignores Mum when she starts rattling on about growing vegetables. Has another beer.

4pm - starts on the wine or occasionally takes the dog for another walk or has another beer.

5pm - more time on the xbox.

6-7pm - dinner.

7.30pm - he usually lies on the sofa bingeing Netflix and ignoring Mum when she tries to discuss what we all want for dinner tomorrow.

Me:

I stay up late on FaceTime with my friends most nights, so I'm really tired in the morning. We all have a lie in and then do our school work in the afternoon. It's much better - if only school started at lunchtime I'm sure we'd all concentrate much better and work harder.

We all sign in to FaceTime and Google Classroom so we can do our work and chat at the same time.

I spend lots of time on TikTok and watch stuff on the iPad and go for a family walk - sometimes just me and Mum go with the dog. I like that. We sit on this hill for a bit where there's a really nice view and sometimes I tell her if I'm worried about anything, but mostly I'll tell her funny stuff I talked about with my friends in the day.

Sometimes I'll watch a programme with Mum and Neville - usually a comedy thing and then I'll go in my room about 9pm to listen to music and make videos and chat to my friends. There's this boy I like called Tom, he lives quite nearby and goes to another school - Em's family know his family quite well, and we've started chatting most nights. I haven't mentioned him to Mum - she'll just ask loads of annoying questions.

So that's pretty much how every day / night goes - apart from Thursday - on Thursday at 8pm we stand on the doorstep and cheer and clap for the NHS. Boris even came out of isolation tonight and stood outside Downing Street - so he can't be that ill. He did say "I'm not allowed out really, I'm just standing here." I suppose that's OK if he's just on his doorstep.

3rd April - Lockdown Day 12

Mum couldn't get a delivery slot for ANY of the dates in the whole of April so she goes to the big Tesco. We haven't bothered checking deliveries for May. There's no point anyway, the last delivery we managed to get in March had 57 missing items and only ended up costing about £15 - and most of that was disgusting vegan sausages that obviously NO ONE else in the country wanted! She was really angry that her quinoa order was substituted with straight-to-wok noodles. That was weird, no idea who'd be hoarding quinoa ...

So instead Mum has decided to keep every other delivery driver in the country as busy as possible by ordering tons and tons of stuff. So much for saving the planet! Delivery vans are turning up ALL DAY and stuff covered in tons of plastic is being thrown on the front lawn. I don't call that ESSENTIAL.

One of the drivers said, "catch - that one's fragile," as he lobbed it all the way from the end of the driveway straight at the front door. Mum shot him one of her looks, so he said, “cheer up darlin', it might never happen" and got back in his van. That annoyed her. She stomped back indoors saying,"there's a deadly virus actually killing everyone and we can't leave the house .. IT literally IS happening."

Apparently I'm not allowed to buy ANY new clothes or make up, because we need all our money for the mortgage and the bills. But she's bought SO much stuff !!!

So far this week this is what's arrived :

Top Soil (in a massive heap on the drive)

Plants

Vegetable seeds

Garden tools

Indoor mini-greenhouse

Outdoor vegetable planter boxes

2 massive buckets of white paint

3 tins of furniture paint

A treadmill

A boxing punch bag

5 boxes of wine

As if she's going to do DIY and grow vegetables !!!

Oh and a Sodastream arrived off of Ebay - someone told her she could make her own Prosecco in it. Neville said, "what … like some kind of modern day quarantined version of Jesus?" That annoyed her.

Neville had 2 barrels of IPA delivered because the pub shut and it was all going to go out of date. He's doing a pretty good job of getting through it quickly. Speaking of the pub shutting, Neville has moved all Mum's meditation cushions and crystals out of the shed and back into the spare room and he's turning the shed into a garden pub. He said it's "a matter of life or death" (bit dramatic) because if he can't go out to the pub, he can at least go out to the garden. I don't care what the shed's used for - if it means he spends less time shouting about the dishwasher I'm all for it.

So while Neville's spending all his time swearing and trying to cut up bits of wood to make a bar, Mum is spending ALL her time eating. She literally eats constantly for the whole day. Although at the moment Neville's sitting in an empty shed with a pint of IPA and Mum's taken a bottle of wine and gone to have a bath in the middle of the day.

It's because they just had a MASSIVE row about the dishwasher. She said he was "mansplaining" about where the bowls should go and he said, "Do you know Jaz, I used to have a recurring nightmare about being trapped in a small space with a fat angry feminist, and thanks to a global f***ing pandemic it seems to be coming true."

5th April - Queen's Speech - Lockdown Day 14

It's gorgeous and sunny out and EVERYONE in the WHOLE world seems to be having a BBQ today. Well .. everyone on our street anyway.

All the BBQ's smell lovely and are making me want a burger for dinner. It's a shame because we haven't got any charcoal. I suggested we get some, but Mum said that "people popping out all the time to buy the odd thing are part of the problem." That's a joke - she'd pop out herself if there was absolutely no alcohol in the house.

Mum is feeling a bit rough. She spent the last two nights sitting in the kitchen with her earphones in, getting plastered over Zoom with her mates. The earphones just make her shout even louder at the screen - I had to turn off the film I was trying to watch in the next room and shut myself in my bedroom. Even then I could still hear her. I don't know if she thinks the microphone doesn't work or what .. Even Grandma can do Zoom better than her …

So now she is sunbathing, drinking Vodka and reading a book - oh and moaning about the fact that she has to drink Vodka because there isn't any Gin to be found anywhere in the town.

Neville is drinking more of his IPA and ranting about the fact that his garden pub was supposed to be just for him. He just marched indoors and shouted, "I wanted to sit and have a peaceful pint, but OH NO… your Mother has decided to splay herself all over a f***ing sunbed, right by the shed door, blasting out some kind of weird sound-wave crap."

I told him that Mum says it's "vibrational healing music, with positive energy frequencies."

But he said, "It's just SH*T Ruby .. healing music my arse …. it's making my ears bleed."

It's officially the Easter holidays and we were supposed to be going away to the coast.

But no-one is going anywhere now.

Thank goodness I can FaceTime all my friends.

Also the Queen is apparently talking to the Nation today on the TV. She only does that at Christmas. I asked Neville why she's doing it now - and if it means that there's something really bad to announce.

Mum said, "Don't worry Ruby, I expect she just wants to officially thank all the NHS staff and the other other key workers for everything they are doing."

But Neville said, “yeah that and bollocking all those idiots that were out having f'ing birthday parties and picnics yesterday. And I hope she mentions the lycra-clad twats that thought cycling in massive packs was a good idea too - I bloody hate those nobs.”

I wonder if she will say how long this is going on for …... I don't suppose anyone knows really. Even the Queen.

It's really weird taking the dog for a walk - you have to shout at people from a distance, and everyone is mowing lawns and painting furniture in their gardens, or taking up jogging.

Neville says if a load of Aliens came down to earth right now they'd think there were two types of humans that exist:

He said, “there's the fitness freaks, obsessed with DIY, ordering sourdough starter kits off the internet and growing their own sodding vegetables. Then there's the fat, drunk TV addicts, spending every waking moment eating snacks, and foraging for alcohol, who are all obsessed with some insane yank with a mullet who breeds tigers.”

The Queen's speech was really nice actually. She said stuff about challenges and succeeding. At the end she said “We should take comfort that, while we may have more still to endure, better days will return: we will be with our friends again; we will be with our families again; we will meet again.” That was the point when Mum burst into tears. That was a bit much - probably the menopause again.

6th April - Lockdown Day 15

I've moved into my room as it was too annoying being the kitchen - either Mum's in there banging around with pots and pans talking about what to make for dinner. Or she's in there trying to bake. Mostly though she's just in there opening the cupboards and the fridge every few minutes, trying to decide what to eat every single hour of the day.

So I'm now doing school work on my bed, because there are no desks available for delivery ANYWHERE at the moment. Uncle Marc had to make one for Auntie Sophie at their house. He found some wood in a skip in London and bought some fancy iron legs from a hardware shop and it looks like a really cool retro desk, the kind that would cost a fortune in the shops near their house.

Neville offered to make one for me - I can only imagine how that would have turned out - Mum is still waiting for him to put 2 shelves up in the bedroom - so I said no thanks. Mum's said she's managed to find a fold away plastic camping table that I can use until desks come back into stock. Even THAT can't be delivered for a week.

I've got loads of school work because of GCSEs, I shouldn't even need to do any since it's the holidays, but I can't even go out and see my friends so I might as well do it. It's really sunny as well. What a crappy Easter holiday.

OMG - and MUM is totally nagging me to tidy my room.

Seriously? There is literally NO POINT. No one is allowed in the house so no one is going to see it. Honestly parents.

7th April - Lockdown Day 16

Boris went to hospital for some tests and now he's in the ICU - that can't be good. Neville says it's probably a publicity stunt and Mum says it's probably so they can keep a closer eye on him.

Mum is writing lists of all the stuff she wants to do in lockdown. If I didn't have to study for my GCSEs I literally wouldn't do anything ! I don't know why people feel they have to do stuff. Mum is on at Neville about all these DIY jobs and saying they should transform the garden and decorate the house. I can tell Neville was thinking he'd just spend a couple of months on the Xbox instead.

People are doing loads of fitness challenges (well .. people that don't live in THIS house are). One man is even climbing the equivalent of Mount Everest up and down his stairs. Insane.

Mum signed up for a running challenge … let's see if THAT comes to anything. Neville said she'd run if the shops were about to shut and she wanted a bottle of wine. He thinks he's SO funny. Idiot.

There are rainbow pictures in everyone's windows and signs thanking the NHS. Little kids have drawn chalk rainbows on the pavements as well. We see lots of them when we are out for our Boris walk. I quite liked the walk for a bit but now I'm so bored of walking the same route every day. I don't go as often as I did before. Sometimes I just put some music on and take the dog out on my own. She hasn't been off the lead for ages in case she runs up to someone and doesn't come back, we might not be able to social distance if she does.

At the start of lockdown Martha was posting pictures all over her social media of perfectly baked banana bread, arts and crafts projects with the kids and endless family bike rides. And talking about the gift of time with the family. That's all kind of stopped in the last week or so. Privately she rings mum in tears most nights saying how awful it is being shut up in the house with Terence day after day and not able to see anyone else. She said he's angry all time and can't stop criticising her. He's started going out for long bike rides with Trevor in the middle of the day instead of making the family all go out cycling and then he works really late into the evening. So now they don't even have time together after the kids go to bed. She said that's easier in some ways.

Lizzy has given up on homeschooling, it was too chaotic with the little kids so now they are doing lots of "sports" studies in the garden, and outdoor cookery lessons on the BBQ and her tan looks really good.

Jane's family have theme nights several times a week. They dress up and the food matches the theme and sometimes they choose a family film that fits with it as well. It looks really fun. Some of the costumes are really clever. I asked Mum why we haven't done anything like that. She said it's because she's taking this time to "pause and rejuvenate" and not put pressure on herself to be productive - this from the woman with the massive list of things that she should do in lockdown.

Honestly I don't think she remembers what she says from one minute to the next.

I think she must have felt a bit guilty because then she said, "we can do theme dinners if you want to Ruby". TBH I didn't so I told her to go back to rejuvenating and not worry about it.

Also .... I still haven't told her that Tom is kind of my boyfriend now and I like talking to him in the evenings - I won't get to do that if I have to spend loads of time having "family fun" with her and Neville.

Tonight we had a family Zoom quiz. Auntie Sophie organised it - she hadn't had a very good day, because Feliz had ruined the herb garden she'd created in a special planter in the garden. Everything had been growing really nicely, with all the good weather, but Felix decided he didn't like the herbs and pulled them all out of the planter and threw them over the fence into next door's garden. Coco came on the screen and said, "Felix had to go on the naughty step for 20 minutes. It's because his behaviour was atrocious." Neville said, "Is that a word from your flip chart," but Coco didn't answer him. She asked me why my hair looked such a mess instead ... Rude.

The quiz didn't last very long. Ella couldn't answer any of the general knowledge questions and wanted to know why there wasn't a "reality TV stars" round. That annoyed Grandpa who said, "why don't you know any general knowledge Ella?"

Auntie Sophie said she was sorry but she doesn't watch reality TV. Then something went on between Felix and Coco and Auntie Sophie had to put BOTH of them on the naughty step so we all abandoned the quiz.

8th April - Lockdown Day 17

Apparently Boris is sitting up in bed and getting a bit better and Mum is now attempting to make Banana Bread. What a waste of time. Neither me or Neville like bananas … maybe that's the whole point. This way she can eat the whole thing without worrying about sharing any of it.

Banana Bread is EVERYWHERE according to Mum. I know Martha made some, but I doubt it's everywhere .. if it is then that's probably why she's trying to make it .. she's always trying to make sure she copies what everyone else is doing.

Mind you .. looks like Martha is losing the plot a bit in lockdown - she's completely stopped posting all the photos of baking and bike rides and puzzles and family walks now. Yesterday she put on a video of herself pouring some wine into a pint glass and saying, "My kids have been little sh*ts today. Have yours? I don't know about you, but I'm going get hammered and watch my Sex and The City boxset .. Cheers …" Then she downed the WHOLE pint of wine in one go.

Neville said, 'blimey .. I didn't think she had it in her," and walked off looking quite impressed.

Update : The banana bread was a disaster .. went straight in the bin.

9th April - Lockdown Day 18

Boris has left intensive care.

Neville is online trying to buy paint from B&Q. He got up this morning and announced that if "every other b***ard in the country" was decorating their house then he might as well do it too.

When he opened the website it said there were nearly 110,000 people in front of him and he would have to wait about an hour in the queue. He shouted something that I really don't want to write here and said, "It's a f***ing joke, it's not like I'm trying to get tickets for sodding Glastonbury."

Mum said that was a stupid thing to say since all the festivals are cancelled.

She'd just got back from a run looking like she was about to have a stroke. It's really hot outside, but she was also really angry because a policeman had stopped her and suggested she was breaking the rules on the amount of time she'd been outside exercising. Apparently he said, "you've obviously been out here running for hours judging by the state of you. People are supposed to be out for short amounts of time, not running marathons."

She had to tell him that she'd only been going for 10 minutes ... Neville thought it was hilarious - he laughed so hard he woke the dog .. she jumped off the sofa petrified, knocked over his laptop and ran into the garden.

When he picked up the laptop he'd lost his place in the queue for the B&Q website and had to start again.

10th April - Lockdown Day 19

The papers are all about Boris getting better and not really talking about all the people that have died. The NHS are complaining that they don't have enough protective clothing.

Mum's getting a bit paranoid if anyone coughs or sniffles. She takes my temperature every day and keeps telling me to get as much sun as possible because Vitamin D is good for Coronavirus.

Debbie started the year convinced the whole family had ALL had Coronavirus, and she wouldn't take no for an answer when she insisted on getting them all tested and they were negative. THEN she was trying to see if they could have an antibody test to show that they'd already had it. Mum said they get every winter bug (and summer one for that matter) so if anyone had had it already it would be that family. Literally every day they've got one symptom or another. Even the ones that are really unusual like upset stomachs and a weird thing to do with your toes.

Neville said, "based on Debbie's description of all their illnesses, she had it before the first case was even RECORDED in China. The woman's an idiot."

11th April - Lockdown Day 20

Priti Patel was on TV today doing her first lockdown briefing .. she must have been nervous, because she said there had been "three hundred thousand and thirty four, nine hundred and seventy four thousand" Coronavirus tests done in Britain. Math's is totally my WORST subject and even I know that's not an actual number. None of these politicians seems to know what they are doing.

It makes me a bit anxious thinking they are making important decisions for us and they all seem confused as well … I tried to talk to Mum about it but she was on Zoom with Margaret having a "Gin tasting experience."

12th April - Lockdown Day 21

Boris came out of hospital and said he owed his life to the NHS … Neville made lots of sarcastic comments about what a coincidence it was that Boris was managing to "rise from the dead" over the Easter weekend.

13th April - Bank Holiday Monday - Lockdown Day 22

Terence Appleby has apparently made a perfect loaf of Sourdough. Neville said, "I might have known that smug git would manage to make one." Martha, said "well, it ought to be good, he's been working on it for long enough. Made him almost as excited as the special new massage oil Trevor bought him - he says it relieves his tired muscles after being on the bike all day. Apparently I don't massage it in properly so Trevor has to do it. Fine with me, if it means he spends less time shouting at me."

14th April - Lockdown Day 23

It's Lizzy's birthday today - Jane & Bridget delivered a food hamper & lots of wine to her house. They made a special cake that looked like a toilet roll - it was pretty funny. They had to go in separate cars and leave it on the doorstep and sing Happy Birthday from over the road. Mum has been in the garden doing Zoom drinks in the sun with all of them for the last two hours. I went to wave at the screen because she told me to. I'm not sure any of them really cared. But Mum said, "come and show everyone your new hair Ruby" They all liked my hair dark, but I told Mum it's fading and I need to dye it again.

Neville - along with the whole of the rest of the world - is STILL trying to make his own Sourdough bread. He's not had much success so far. There's a massive jar of this stinky beige stuff in the kitchen, which has just exploded out of the jar and is all over the dresser that Mum "upscaled" two days ago. She will be furious when she finishes her Zoom call.

Neville managed to scrape it all off, but the starter thing is like sticky cement and it's taken half the paint off the dresser. I think Neville should re-paint it for her. I was about to say as much, but he was trying to get the gloopy sticky stuff off his hands and wasn't listening. I went off to my room, just as he shouted, "F**k you Paul Hollywood" and smashed the mason jar thing into the bin.

15th April - Lockdown - Day 24

Today it is actually over a MONTH since we started staying home - we are about 10 days ahead of other people because Mum made us start early, but it wasn't properly official until 23rd March after all the pubs shut.

The days are sort of blurring into each other now - Neville keeps saying we know when it's a Thursday because people clap outside and we know when it's Sunday because the bins go out. Other than that it's ALL the same ….

It's been really sunny so the Easter holiday went really, really fast .. every day has been sunny. We've eaten loads of chocolate, had 3 BBQs, and gone on LOADS of dog walks. Neither Mum or Neville appear to be doing any work anymore - although Mum writes lots of pointless lists and then just lies about on the sofa for most of the day. I'm the only one actually doing anything productive.

Lots more people have died which is really scary, but the news has mostly been about Boris getting better and leaving hospital.

Mum is still running now and again - even after the embarrassing thing with the policeman the other day. She is on about keeping fit while she's in lockdown, but she gave up on Joe Wicks after about 2 days. Mind you I can't talk, I haven't even done ONE day of Joe Wicks workouts. But then I didn't choose to take Sport as a GCSE, so I don't think I should have to do anything.

Mum says that's irrelevant and everyone should be doing exercise for their immune system. The amount of wine she's drinking I reckon she must be immune to most things anyway.

Neville suggested she do some of Ollie's online workouts since she's always banging on about being a vegan. He's started calling Ollie "The Joe Wicks of Lentils." He's just jealous. Ollie's subscriber list is massive and he's being interviewed for podcasts and all sorts.

So when Mum isn't banging about immune systems, she's banging on about us all starting new hobbies during lockdown. I'm totally not interested … and Neville says if she thinks he's learning to speak Mandarin and taking up the Ukulele she can forget it.

Mums hobbies are:

Running, now and again, and coming back with a REALLY purple face;
Saying she's going to start doing 30 days of Yoga with Adrienne on YouTube every day and then not actually doing it;
Saying she's going to "write her memoir" and then not actually doing it (massive relief - who'd be interested in that … seriously ??)
Drinking more than usual;
Eating more than usual;
Attempting to paint watercolour pictures (they are beyond TERRIBLE);
Shouting at her friends on Zoom with a glass in her hand;
Shouting at people from a distance on dog walks.

Neville's hobbies are :
Drinking Beer;
Going on the X-box;
Arguing with Mum.

To be honest Neville's hobbies have barely changed. Mum however is obsessed with Zoom drinks parties. There's now a Fizz Friday & Wine Saturday and Gin & Tonic nights on any other random occasion she can find. She doesn't realise that the microphone works fine and she can just talk normally. She spends hours screaming at the screen and cackling really loudly. It's SO annoying.

Also she keeps saying we should be doing TikTok dances together …. so embarrassing. I am so sick of hearing "Come on Ruby, loads of other Mums are doing it - it will be fun." Other Mums are probably good at it and not as irritating as she is. Yesterday she even said, "Don't be such a misery Ruby .. we might become TikTok famous."

OH.MY.GOD … totally deluded.

To be honest though she's not the only one. Auntie Sophie had to disable Uncle Marc's TikTok account because she said he'd turned into "one of those embarrassing middle-aged Dads."

Right now Mum is in the kitchen, sitting in front of her laptop AGAIN, with a bottle of Prosecco and a massive bowl of pickled onions shouting at Bridget, Helen and Jane. She just yelled at me, "It's virtual happy hour .." Seems like the whole day is virtual happy hour right now.

If Mum is an embarrassing idiot, then Neville is even worse. He just put a Chemical Banana Zoom rehearsal online …. PUBLICLY!! It's him and his idiot band mates playing their terrible songs in 4 separate spare bedrooms, because they think their "fans" are missing them playing live. Him thinking they have an actual fanbase that misses them is worse than Mum thinking she can do TikTok dancing …..

He just said, "That was absolutely f***ing legendary stuff Ruby .. I'm off to the pub for a post-gig beer with the lads," and then he took his laptop into the shed.

The two of them are SO SAD.

I seriously hope this lockdown won't be as long as people are saying .. my mental health will be severely damaged …..

17th April - Lockdown Day 26

Friday is our shopping day. They make an absolutely MASSIVE deal of the shopping. They say it's because they are only allowed to shop when necessary so they have to make sure to get everything at once. That's crap for a start - they are always popping out for this and that (usually wine) - though sometimes it's to get treats for me! It takes forever to do the shop because you have to queue outside 2 metres apart, and then disinfect the trolley. There's only one member of the family at a time allowed in as well - which suits me because it means I can't get dragged along on one of Mums "you need to get some fresh air" missions. Then you have to walk around the shop really carefully following the one way signs and not getting near other people.

Uncle Dave and Auntie Sally are doing Grandma and Grandpa's shopping, because they have to isolate. Auntie Sally makes them order by a certain time, then she stays up late for new click & collect slots to become free and then she puts the orders in her and for Grandma and Grandpa. Then she goes and collects it all on the day she picked and brings it all home and disinfects everything and takes it round to Grandma's house. Sometimes she leaves it on the doorstep and they talk through the window for a few minutes. If it's a nice day she takes a flask of tea and sits in the garden and they talk through a crack in the patio doors. I think that would make me sad. We haven't seen them for about 6 weeks now which is really strange. Mum said we will drive over sometime, go through the side gate and sit in the garden so we don't have to touch anything . But it makes me really sad that I can't give them a hug so I prefer to FaceTime them or ring for a chat.

Mind you I rang Grandma for a chat today, but she was about to have a Zoom book club meeting and didn't have time to talk to me.

So, a couple of days ago, I said Neville's hobbies are pretty much the same as they've always been ..... that's actually NOT TRUE.

He HAS got a new hobby .... he has decided to start a YouTube Channel to do his ranting on. It's a total nightmare !!

He's been ranting absolutely non-stop the last few days ... there's been soooooo much stuff annoying him so now it's all online. This is worse than Chemical Banana videos. His channel is called "Do One Boris."

I told him that literally NO ONE will watch videos of him just ranting at a screen .. but he said it's "topical political satire" like on Mock the Week and people love it especially at times like this. I tried to tell him that Mock the Week has actual comedians on it who are funny, but he wasn't listening. He was going to wear a Chemical

Banana baseball hat to start with but he's ordered a T-shirt and cap that match instead. They both say "Do One Boris" on the front.

He's really chuffed with himself and has just been in and left the first effort open on his ipad for me to watch ….. He put on a note on top saying "Hi Ruby, thought I'd record some of my thoughts about the pandemic. If I die from the 'rona then I want you to make sure you share this from YouTube to everywhere you can .. keep my memory alive and show the world what I think… PS: It was fun .. I might make more videos.

OMG.

Alright there - I'm Neville, part of the band Chemical Banana .. you might have heard of us. Anyway, as well as putting out a bit of excellent rock music from time to time, I also have a wife Jaz who is into all sorts of spiritual crap - she's probably doing some meditation ritual as we speak, most likely from some fake online druid that's convinced her to part with some money for his "instructional videos". And I've got a daughter Ruby, who is holed up in her room for hours these days making endless TikTok videos, so I barely see her.

*So whilst she's trying to get TikTok famous, and the wife is busy falling for whatever the latest snake oil might be, I thought I'd try a bit of video and tell all of you some of my thoughts about this current sh*tshow of a situation .. who knows I might go viral yet ! (get it .. viral ..haahha).*

So share with your mates and let me know your thoughts down below (points at the bottom of the screen).

So I will tell you what my main thoughts are ..

First - COVIDIOTS in the shops !! How hard is it to walk round a shop, following a set of arrows? Aye? There's always someone going in the wrong direction. It's not like it's rocket science. Yesterday 2 people barged right past me like there isn't an actual PANDEMIC going on and another covidiot leaned right over my trolley to get himself a pineapple. Couldn't wait 2 f'ing seconds until I moved on.

Oh and at least 4 people were walking around coughing. What the hell ?? Why weren't they at home? What is wrong with people.

Second - PENSIONERS!! Seriously I've had enough of pensioners .. the very people we are supposed to be protecting are out there, standing around chatting to one another and not even TRYING to observe social distancing rules..

I just took the dog out for a walk and literally had to shout at this old woman. She came and stood right next to me at the traffic lights so I gave her what for. I yelled, "Two metres, yes YOU ... yes I'm talking to you! Get back ...TWO METRES ... !!!!!" Pretty much every day there's some old git out there that I have to remind about the rules. Jaz says it's totally uncalled for, but what's the point in rules if people aren't even following them.

*Finally. Exercise. 1 hour of exercise it's meant to be. Susan from No. 19 is out 3 or 4 times a day. She came round yesterday wondering if she could borrow the dog from time to time to get her out of the house. It's madness. On which subject LOADS of people are ignoring the 1 hour rule and going out for longer. HOW to I know?? F***ing Strava maps uploaded to social media. I see you Susan .. I know what you are doing.*

So people posting their Strava maps can DO ONE; people not social distancing can DO ONE and anyone that can't follow an f'ing arrow painted on the ground can definitely DO ONE.

What rubbish … hopefully one of two things will happen, no-one will watch and Neville will get disheartened or his furlough will finish and he won't have time…. Sadly I don't think furlough will end for ages …

One of the weirdest things about lockdown (apart from Neville suddenly getting into YouTube) is everyone worrying about everyone else's behaviour. People have turned into the COVID Police!!

Susan going out and about several times a day has been noticed by Derek for a start, Neville said it's been mentioned in the neighbours WhatApp group. He also wrote "Sally, I noticed you going through the side gate into Mr Davis's garden yesterday. We aren't supposed to visit other people." Turned out Sally was apparently dropping off some homemade banana bread as a gift. Mr Davis had to supply photographic evidence to shut Derek up.

I don't know why Neville has such a thing about Pensioners, he's always made comments about them (usually related to the ones that read The Daily Mail) but never used to actually SHOUT at them in public.I really like old people. Literally EVERYONE ELSE is being EXTRA NICE to old people, making sure they are OK and doing their shopping for them and stuff like that. I think he's just bored and wants to have a go at someone.

Mum thinks he's in a bad mood because his Chemical Banana rehearsal video didn't get a single like or comment on it. He just said, "Don't talk bollocks Janice … it went down a storm. My DMs were blowing up."

So embarrassing .. can't believe he said that.

The only pensioner he does actually like at the moment is Captain Tom Moore who has been walking up and down his garden to raise millions for the NHS.

Me and Mum both cried when he did the last lap and the TV filmed it. I'm going to send him a 100th Birthday card.

18th April - Lockdown Day 27

The dog absolutely loves us all being home - she's so happy. She's going to be really sad when everyone goes back to normal. She has got a new activity tracker called a Pit Pat - it records calories, how much sleep she's had and stuff like that. It also has "walking" "playing" and "pottering" settings.Yesterday she did 8 and a half hours of pottering.

Seriously, she's like an old person. Grandma said if Grandpa had a Pit Pat he'd have a really really high pottering score too.

If I had the lockdown equivalent of a Pit Pat tracker it would have settings like:

* lying on the bed bored;
* watching YouTube;
* looking for non-existent snacks in the kitchen;
* making TikTok videos;
* shutting the bedroom door so I can't hear Mum shouting drunkenly on Zoom;
* finding stuff on Disney+ that I used to watch when I was a kid;
* avoiding school work.

Speaking of mum shouting on Zoom .. it's a "Girls catch up night." Last night was "Fizz Friday Virtual Drinks" again … I'm sure that was only two days ago .. either I'm losing track of time or she's just adding extra drinking dates into her diary. I've asked Neville for some noise-cancelling headphones - hopefully Amazon will still be able to deliver them.

I used to have sleepovers with friends on the weekends .. we'd cook pizzas, eat loads of sweets and talk about which boys we liked. That seems a long time ago. Last time we did that all the boys still had proper haircuts instead of skinheads … some have grown out a bit and look terrible, others have shaved them again and they all look terrible too…..

There was just a massive shout from the kitchen - Neville has just thrown another Sourdough starter in the bin.

19th April - Lockdown Day 28

In America there are tons of people not following lockdown. They are out on the streets protesting that Covid is a hoax. Neville and Uncle John keep messaging each other memes about it and using words like ‘retard,’ ‘moron’ and Covidiot.

There are lots of new words now .. Covidiot is one, Spaffer (usually used when people are talking about Boris) and of course “unprecedented.” Everyone is using that one EVERY SINGLE TIME they talk about anything to do with Corona.

Oh and tonight we got dinner from the chip shop. Neville decided to have cod instead of 2 battered sausages … that was pretty unprecedented ..

It made a bit of a change, so I was actually a bit excited. How sad is that?

20th April - Lockdown Day 29

School officially started back today - but of course we are all still at home - only the kids of key workers actually go to school. There’s a bunch of stuff ready for us in Google Classroom, I don’t really want to work through it, but I haven’t got much choice. Even when I’m following my school timetable all the days just blend into each other.

Mum swops between days of getting up late, wandering around in PJs, crying occasionally, and then lying on the sofa watching Netflix. Other days are those where she’s up early, going running, making cupcakes, painting bits of furniture and sitting on the computer writing blogs about spiritual nonsense.

She’s had no work at all and is thinking of retraining to be a hypnotherapist … oh god .. see where that goes - she said has natural healing energy - no idea where she gets that idea from. She said, “fundamentally I’m an empath with natural skills in nurturing and comforting people. So if people are emotionally or physically in a bad place, I’m able to sooth and rebalance them.” Honestly. She must think I’m an idiot. Whenever I feel ill she just tells me to stop making a fuss and get over it. I wouldn't exactly call that nurturing and comforting.

24th April - Lockdown Day 33

So yesterday was really, really bad (and by bad I mean A LOT of money went in the swear jar) because President Trump has been making statements about how we could try and defeat the virus. He was talking about UV light and then said that maybe we could try injecting people with disinfectant to stop the Coronavirus. Auntie Mindy (she's my Cousin Jamie's Mum in America) said that the big detergent companies are having to bring out official statements and Ad campaigns telling people not to inject bleach and other disinfectants into themselves …

It's completely mad. Neville is stomping around the house calling him a "deranged Tangerine Sh*tgibbon."

Meanwhile everyone is posting pictures of themselves on social media pretending to drink bottles of Dettol and Toilet Duck. Mum put a photo of herself drinking in the garden and wrote, "Cheers everyone .. Zoflora and soda in the sunshine - UV AND disinfectant all in one go. We aren't taking any chances with the virus in this house."

Neville said, "Trump's got a little bit of a point though Jaz .. if you are injecting Cillit Bang into yourself it probably won't be Covid that kills you."

Mum has basically been trying to drink and sunbathe her way through everything and try to take no notice of the news, but the disinfectant thing seemed to wind her up a bit. She said the shops have only just got all the cleaning products back in stock after all the panic buying, and this will probably make it worse again. Neville said It will only make it worse if people are "actual f***ing retards and they listen to anything that "moron with the tiny little hands" has to say.

Most of the time though Mum is really chilled out and happy. She's spending lots of time relaxing, reading books and going on and on about how blue the sky is without all the pollution. How peaceful it is everywhere without the traffic. She keeps banging on to me about nature and how powerful it is and how "the only thing you can hear outside is the amazingly loud birdsong everywhere." She just came in from the garden looking all calm and said, "It's just amazing Ruby - it's like all the sounds of Mother Earth's true personality are finally getting through to the human race … listen to the birds out there .. it's just like a beautiful soundtrack of universal peace."

Neville was in the middle of stuffing his face with a massive piece of cake and said (between mouthfuls) .. "Peace Jaz? Peace? All you can hear from dawn to dusk is lawnmowers, jet washers, sanders, drills and every single bloody power tool known to man. I would absolutely love to have no noise to listen to apart from all the sh**ting birds."

He's a fine one to talk about noise - it's bin day tomorrow. Last week the sound of the men emptying our bottle recycling into the van almost drowned out the sound of the dog barking at them. Neville's had to replace our grey glass recycling box with a massive plastic dustbin because there are SO MANY bottles …. it took 2 of the bin men to actually lift it into the van.

SO EMBARRASSING !

25th April - Lockdown Day 34

Neville here. So where are we with this whole global pandemic right now?

Firstly - we haven't shut any borders - we are an f'ing island - that's SOMETHING we could actually do ! But NO .. there are plane loads of people just turning up at the airports, there's no checks or tests, and then they just get on public transport, or into cars and taxis and head off wherever ... spreading the virus all over the country. What's the point in your Auntie Madge taking all the precautions to *stay safe, when some idiot can come back from a holiday in Spain and just go straight to Tescos.. A load of the people that are coming in are fruit pickers from Romania - most of them left because of Brexit but (surprise surprise) it turns out Brits don't want to pick fruit 'cos it's a sh*tty job, so the farmers have had to persuade the Romanians to come back again ...*

Trump .. don't get me started on that twat - he thinks he's some kind of medical genius - suggesting people drink disinfectant or have ultra violet lights shined up their backsides to kill the virus!

That colossal twat Matt Hancock has decided that care workers aren't going to be getting a pay rise, but they are all going to get a nice little badge to wear. That's alright then ! Who needs money to pay the bills aye, why not put your life on the line for a crappy bit of metal. What a kick in the teeth.

And talking of people putting their life on the line - we are all doing the Thursday night clapping for the NHS - and on the TV they are showing a massive group of people all wedged together on tower bridge - videoing themselves clapping standing next to other people. What's the point???

*Oh yeah ... and wait for this... that nasty smirking witch Priti Patel was on TV. She looked very pleased with herself and said during the virus outbreak incidents of shop-lifting, burglary and car theft were much lower. No sh*t Sherlock .. what with shops being shut and people being home all day. There are probably fewer injuries from pub fights, accidents where people get scalded with hot coffee in Starbucks and a decrease in theme park accidents as well .....*

Priti Patel? Priti vacant more like .. she's a vacuous waste of space that woman.

Oh and finally I STILL can't get on the B&Q website.

*So yeah. Do one Boris, Do one Priti Patel, and DO ONE B and f**king Q !*

It's terrible about the care workers. The ones that look after Neville's Dad are lovely and they DEFINITELY deserve a pay rise. Another person has died in the Care Home where Neville's dad is. That's 7 this week. He can still only talk to his Dad on FaceTime because no one is allowed to visit. They are trying to make it nice for the people there by letting them sit out in the garden for a bit. Neville's Dad is OK for now, but it's really worrying.

And as for Priti Patel, even I know those figures mean absolutely nothing since it's pretty hard to shoplift when the shops are shut!

I thought politicians were supposed to be clever. Mind you Neville spat his tea out when I said that.

26th April Lockdown Day - Day 35

Today would have been the London Marathon. It's really hot today and it's been really sunny ALL week. Loads of people are really disappointed - I can imagine it's a real shame if you've spent months and months training. Some people are going out and running it in their local towns and some people are even running 26 miles in a circle around their garden … that must be SO boring!!

There's been clear blue skies and perfect weather every single day and we are having loads of BBQs. It kind of feels like a really lovely summer holiday - except lots of people are dying and I still can't visit Grandma and Grandpa. Also I have to do school work every day.

Some days it's fine and other days it's just really weird that this is even happening.

Uncle Marc had his 40th Birthday over the weekend, so we all did a Zoom call and had a drink with him. Well I didn't have one, but everyone else did even though it was 11 o'clock in the morning. On his actual Birthday they did lots of fun stuff all day so he could forget that it was Lockdown and he couldn't go to the Pub. One thing was a Zoom quiz with his friends from all around the World.

There was a true or false round where people had to guess if Uncle Marc had done various things.

To be honest he's done SO many stupid things that I would always answer yes to anything that sounded ridiculous enough for him to have done it. One was whether he once tried to cook frozen fish fingers in the toaster when he came in drunk one night. OBVIOUSLY that was a yes. Auntie Sophie was a bit annoyed, because when it happened, the smoke alarm woke Coco and Felix up at three in the morning. Felix was really small and had only just gone back to sleep after about 4 hours of screaming. When Auntie Sophie got downstairs to tell him to stop it, he was just about to try boiling an egg in the kettle. She put the fish finger box back in the freezer and unplugged the toaster, and was just about to send him off to bed, but he'd already passed out on the sofa.

Neville has been particularly angry and ranty this week. He's a really weird mixture of being relaxed, because he doesn't have to work and can drink in his man shed all day, and then very angry when people don't do the lockdown the way he wants the lockdown to be done.

He keeps coming back from long dog walks complaining that people are out for long dog walks. And he keeps going out to buy cans of beer and snacks when he's run out and coming back swearing and complaining that people are in the supermarket buying "non essentials" like wine and Pringles.

Honestly.

Oh and Mum seems to have cottoned on that I'm up late chatting to Tom. Sometimes she even wanders in my room without knocking and sees him on the screen. I totally don't want all the questions so I've just told her he's a "friend."

27th April - Lockdown Day 36

People's DIY obsessions seem to be carrying on .. Neville went out to get paint and came back really unhappy because there were so many people trying to get paint … it's a bit of a thing with him. He was moaning about people buying loads of power tools, but today a drill arrived from Amazon. When I pointed that out to him, he said, "well that's different … your Mother wants me to put some shelves up, so she has somewhere to store her 2 million books about self-improvement. And I've needed a decent drill for ages." Then he said, "Speaking of tools that twat Appleby's just been on a 50 mile bike ride .. 50 miles !! Saw it on his Strava map. That's not a 1 hour government exercise is it??"

Then he went off to record a YouTube episode.

Neville here…. We are getting in the swing of the lockdown now but I have to tell you, there are COVIDIOTS EVERYWHERE ! It's driving me crazy.

There are literally so many people not following the rules :

*Cyclists: Let's start there. 1 hour exercise it says.. 1 hour. So if you are off for 4 hours at a time, wedged into a lycra outfit that's too damn small for you a) you look like a d*ck and b) that's breaking the rules.*

And the other day .. listen to this … the other day I saw a whole family in the park - 5 of them - who'd created their own private cycling track. Yep. Commandeered a WHOLE section of the pavement in a PUBLIC park, like they owned the place. Timing laps, and checking stopwatches, literally not noticing anyone else that wanted to use the pavement. Just tearing up and down. I saw at least three old people forced off the path INTO THE MUD to avoid them. Unbelievable.

Runners: Don't get me started on those twats. Running past you, not distancing, sweat flying around, heavy breathing right next to you. Selfish.

Families: Especially big families, all walking 4 a-breast on the pavement. Just stop. Get yourselves into single file will you? Stop taking up the WHOLE pavement.

People complaining about other people's situations: There's all the people working from home complaining that the people on furlough are just on a paid holiday. Then there's the people who are being made redundant complaining about how the people working from home shouldn't be complaining about anything, because they've still got a job. There's all the people with kids complaining about how hard it is to homeschool their kids. And the people without kids saying the people with the kids at home should be "cherishing every moment" and "they'll never get the opportunity again." Tell that to stressed out parents trying to do their full time jobs AND work out how to help their kid with maths.

But then again someone living alone ... in a totally silent house? Well, they might actually welcome a couple of feral kids.

Everyone thinks everyone else has it easier than them, and then people get angry with people who are loving the lockdown and the people who are loving the lockdown are fed up with people who are complaining about the lockdown. And round and round we go.

Finally there's the "It's all a hoax" lot, the "there's no virus it's the government trying to control you" lot. Don't get me started on them and their "WAKE UP SHEEPLE" posts. Ask an ICU nurse if it's real that's what I say - they'll soon tell you!

That's me for today .. So Keep 2 metres apart, take turns giving people space on the pavements (especially if you are a sweaty runner) and live and let live. We are all in different positions - we are all struggling in different ways and none of us chose any of this .. so just BE NICE.

28th April - Lockdown Day 37

TODAY WAS A TOTAL DRAMA !!

I actually went in a car for the first time in like FOREVER .. we had to drive to the hairdressers to get some dye. The box of hair dye that

Mum ordered right at the start of lockdown turned up this morning. So I re-did my hair and it totally came out GINGER !!!! It looked terrible !! I was in absolute floods of tears, Mum just kept saying, "It's fine Ruby, it's a nice auburn colour." It's not. It's ginger. I was in such a state she rang the hairdresser and we drove to her house. She looked at it from a distance and sorted out some colour, and explained how to mix it up and passed it to us over the fence.

So I sorted it and it looked SO MUCH better. But it was still a bit late .. the girls have ALL changed my name in their phones to Ron Weasley !

Mum laughed loads at that. I suppose it's quite funny actually.

Matt Hancock was on TV again. He's the Health Secretary so that makes sense he should be telling us what's going on .. but he always just looks a bit confused.

Quite a few NHS staff have died now - which is SO sad. They are working SOOOO hard to help people. Neville calls him Hatt Mancock so now I keep getting it mixed up as well. There's loads of stuff in the papers about a lack of equipment and people having to re-use PPE - which isn't safe. Some of it isn't even proper equipment to start with - nurses and doctors are just wearing plastic bags which is really terrible. The pictures from China are totally different - they are wearing, like, these full protective suits. They look like something out of a Sci Fi film.

Boris is rattling on about defeating the Coronavirus and called it an "invisible mugger" and said some nonsense about wrestling it. Neville said he knows a bloke that was in intensive care in the middle of March and is still really struggling so he totally doesn't believe Boris even had the virus. He said, "It was probably a PR stunt to make him look like a man of the people."

Mum keeps showing me internet videos of "animals reclaiming nature" whilst all the humans are stuck at home. There were elephants playing on the beach somewhere exotic and dolphins in the Venice canals, where the water is all clear now. Some of the stuff turned out to be fake and not where they said it was at all. So there weren't actually dolphins, but the canals are definitely clearer now that there are no boats and cruise ships and millions of tourists. Mum keeps on about how much pollution has cleared from the skies above countries like China because the factories are closed and there are so few planes flying. Neville keeps making fun of her. He put one of her wooden hippos that she got in Africa in the garden and took a photo of it. Then he posted it on her facebook timeline and wrote, "The animals are reclaiming our garden Jaz."

He's not funny.

29th April - Lockdown Day 38

Boris's girlfriend had their baby today. Lots of people made jokes about it because apparently Boris has lots of children, but he might not be sure how many … how do you NOT know how many kids you've got? Seriously?

Neville was reading comments off of Twitter and chuckling .. he said "David Baddiel wrote Congratulations to Boris Johnson on the birth of his 187th child." I liked David Baddiel on Taskmaster, but Neville always just calls him that git that wrote "football's coming home.." He's still hurt that everyone hated the Chemical Banana spoof version "it's staying there." It's not David Baddiel's fault that Neville's band has no talent.

Speaking about babies Mrs Whitaker is having her baby anytime now so she came on a special Zoom lesson today to say goodbye. We are getting someone called Mr Meeble .. what a ridiculous name .. I just bet he will be "Feeble Meeble" within days. He will also be the 9th RS teacher I've had since I've been at Springfield. I don't know why they leave all the time …. I mean it's not the most exciting subject, but if you've decided to teach RS you must like it surely?

30th April - Lockdown Day 39

So Captain Tom is 100 today and he's raised 32 million pounds for the NHS!! I couldn't watch it on the news because I might have cried - he's so cute.

Lots of people are doing their own challenges to honour his birthday. Neville said his personal challenge was to walk 100 metres to his "Garden Pub" and have several beers.

I told him that wasn't exactly a challenge since he does that every day, but he said, "well it's not exactly a challenge to grow a moustache in November either is it?? or to give up f***ing drinking in January." Well to be honest THAT obviously IS a challenge since he's failed to do it 2 years in a row !!

I tried to say that, but he was still talking, "there are enough knobs that expect me to contribute to their Just Giving Pages. They can repay the favour and sponsor me a few quid to get twatted in my shed."

The sun has disappeared and it's been raining for 2 days - everything is just more depressing when it rains.

Mum and Neville are just on different planets right now. Mum seems to be loving the lockdown and Neville absolutely hates it.

Neville seems to just hate everything that people are doing - and especially what they are sharing on social media. He ranted at me for about an hour earlier - I was trying to do some painting from a YouTube tutorial to relax …

He said, "do you want to know all the things that are annoying me Ruby?" I didn't and told him to go away and rant about it on his "Do ONE Boris!" channel.

Unfortunately he did ..

Right people Neville here .. I dunno ... with every day that goes by there's more stuff on social media to do my head in. Ruby says maybe I should just not look at it .. but I have to keep up with the news, so I can keep you lot up to date. Talking of you lot .. great to see the reviews coming in, keep on sharing this round.

Right what or who can "Do ONE" this week??

Well Matt Hancock for starters ... promised we'd be reaching (sorry "ramping up to") 100,000 tests a day by the end of April. Guess what ? We aren't managing that .. shocker! We did 52,000 the other day and about 70,000 today. They keep trying to say the "capacity" for 100,000 tests is the same as actually DOING 100,000 tests. Maybe if I say I have the "capacity" to get a 1st Class Maths degree I'll get a promotion ... so, yeah ... Do ONE Hancock!

What else .....

** People's lists of stuff on facebook - they really annoy me. I don't give a sh*t about your top 10 albums ... or your favourite films, or your book covers with no explanation. Piss off!*

** People's photos of their daughter or son, or Mother or their bleedin' great Auntie Madge. "Share a photo to flood facebook with positivity." Do ONE! I'm not interested.*

** Photos of people when they were 20 - I don't give a sh*t what you used to look like. You just want me to say you haven't changed. Of course you've changed you deluded idiot - you are MUCH older and MUCH fatter, you have TONS and TONS more wrinkles and you look like you've died inside. DO ONE!*

** People's photos of their home baked goodies. F**k right off. The shops are full of cakes - you don't have to make it yourself and last I heard Mr Kipling is still in business - you can stick the local choir's version of Bake Off up your arse.*

Now Jaz on the other hand - she loves all that. Sharing photos, sharing your favourite things. She's been going on about how wonderful it is to see old albums she'd forgotten about, and pictures of people years ago before she knew them and she's busy asking everyone for their cake recipes. That's a waste of time since she never bakes anything. The Banana bread incident was pretty much a one off !

Jaz's facebook is FULL of positive hashtags like #blessed, #grateful and #livingmybestlifeinlockdown

I told Ruby, "of course your Mother's living her best life, she's spent the last 4 days lying on the sofa with several bottles of Prosecco and a mountain of chocolate watching Downtown bloody Abbey."

So yeah .. Facebook lists .. they can just DO ONE!! Until next time, over and out.

Honestly ! What an idiot.

Anyway - he knows Mum has always loved those kinds of programmes .. they are called "Period Dramas," which I do find a bit of a weird name. But anyway - I don't see why it matters what she likes to watch, he should just stop moaning about it. He said, "No thanks Ruby. All those twats wearing big fancy hats and saying stuff like "have you breakfasted yet?" I'd rather eat a plate of maggots than watch that crap."

I didn't say he had to WATCH it. I just said he should STOP MOANING. He's soooooo annoying. And he totally WOULD NOT eat a plate of maggots - he couldn't cope with cleaning the bin last summer when a bunch of them appeared in there because it was so hot. And he gets really squeamish when "I'm a Celebrity" is on and they do the bushtucker stuff.

1st May - Lockdown Day 40 !!!!

It's another new month and everything is EXACTLY the same. Neville is STILL getting paid to do nothing.

He was complaining today because building sites are all open and builders are allowed to all spend time together. He said, "So if all my friends and family became builders temporarily, we could actually spend time together .. but I'm STILL not allowed to see my OWN Dad. It's RIDICULOUS .. all these rules make NO SENSE. And if all these builders are getting to go to work .. how come there's no sign of those 40 new hospitals they were supposed to be providing? It's crazy.

I get what he's saying about hospitals, but otherwise I really don't understand why he moans so much.

He is basically on HOLIDAY.

Mum is pretty much on holiday as well. The weather is lovely every day and the two of them do nothing but complain. So we have to stay at home - it's not that bad. If anyone should be moaning it's me - I have to do an essay about MacBeth this afternoon.

EVERY SINGLE DAY Mum says, "We are so lucky to have a garden, this must be very hard for people that don't have a garden" … and Neville replies, "I know Jaz, imagine being in a flat with a couple of toddlers."

EVERY SINGLE DAY Neville says, "We've been so lucky with the weather, this would have been much harder if the weather hadn't been so nice" … and Mum replies. "I know Neville, imagine if this had happened over winter."

And then there's the food conversation .. what does anyone want for dinner or lunch or breakfast .. or dinner tomorrow, when no one has made a decision about today yet.

Then Neville will say, “I reckon I should give the Sourdough another go.”
And Mum will say, “I still haven’t made a start on my novel.”

Then one or other will say .. “fancy a drink tonight?” As if it’s something unusual and they don’t do it every night of the week …..

OMG.

Since it’s a Friday Auntie Sophie organised another family Zoom quiz for us .. it was good fun and was going pretty well until Grandmas computer started doing a load of updates that were going to take 45 minutes .. she couldn’t work out how to stop it so we had to abandon the whole thing.

Ever since the Coronavirus started they’ve been going on and on about the “peak” .. apparently we are past that now. It’s supposed to be a good thing.

2nd May - Lockdown Day 41

Neville is spending most of his day blocking people that are plastering social media with conspiracy theories .. apparently these are ..

*5G is going to kill us;
*Bill Gates is making a Covid vaccine that will put microchips into us and track us wherever we go and everyone will be vaccinated by force;
*Coronavirus isn’t real .. it’s invented by the “New Order” whatever that is;
*We are all sleepwalking and allowing the world’s governments to control us and take away our rights.

Mums is blocking people too! The BIG news is, that after two years of obsessing, Mum has now muted Debbie’s account AND Jasmine’s account.

This happened because Mum did a massive speech about how she's trying to fill her world with positivity and that what we absorb from the media is really important. She said, "I only want to have people on my timeline that inspire me and nourish my creative soul." I pointed out if that's the case, then she needs to remove BOTH Debbie and Jasmine from her social media since the pair of them just make her really annoyed, in different ways, and that just isn't in the least bit positive. OMG …it took a serious amount of persuading, but she had to admit it was the best thing to do. Now she can stop being irritated by Debbie and jealous of Jasmine. We will see how long she lasts!

She then made a big announcement that she felt it was time to change her word of the year. She said, "Well obviously, I was really feeling the word FREEDOM at the start of the year, and I felt aligned to that given the new decade and the exciting energy around us. But given we are as good as locked in our houses, it no longer seems appropriate and my new word has finally been revealed to me."

I said I thought "locked in our houses" was a bit of an exaggeration, but that .. yes … Freedom was definitely not suitable.

Then she put on a voice like she's an actress or something and said, 'Well, I have decided my new Word of the Year will be ….. [this was one of those great big dramatic pauses that are just a bit too long, like they use on stuff like Britain's Got Talent] …….. NOURISH."

Neville said, "spot on Jaz .. perfect choice." She looked really pleased until he added, "after all, you've done nothing but eat this year so far."

3rd May - Lockdown Day 42

Today didn't start that well as Mum was pretty angry with Neville after the eating comment. It's not like he's exactly the picture of fitness and health!

She spent two hours on the phone this morning with Martha complaining about him, while Martha complained about Terence. I told Mum you can't really compare them to one another. Neville says stuff because he thinks it's funny .. not because he's trying to be mean. Terence is pretty mean. Martha was only able to talk for so long because he was out with Trevor again. They left early with the bikes and had been gone for hours.

Mum came off the phone and seemed a bit happier. She said to Neville, "at least you make a bit of an effort. Terence is getting worse .. Martha says he's moved into the spare room permanently. He's pretending it's because he works until really late at night, but she knows it's not just that. She thinks he might have someone else on the side."

Neville said, "someone else? That would be impressive, how would you manage to carry on an affair in lockdown? It's pretty unlikely."

They opened a bottle of wine and seemed much happier. Neville had also redeemed himself a bit by getting a fancy roast dinner delivered to the door, including a mushroom wellington thing for Mum. Then later we all watched a funny film together.

7th May - Lockdown Day 46

It's Em's Birthday - and it's just the weirdest thing that we can't see each other properly - she's just turned 15 because of when she was born. I'm one of the oldest in the year (apart from Alice who is right at the start of the new school year so she's always the oldest). We did a Birthday Zoom since that's what all the adults are doing - which was a bit odd. We've always had birthday's together. I'm missing seeing people actually THERE and not on a screen ! It was really funny though and I think she enjoyed it - they were having a family dinner later and she got a gorgeous cake and loads of presents. I dropped her present on her doorstep and waved from the end of the drive. That was weird. No hugs.

Derek and Doreen are out decorating their house for VE day. Derek is up a ladder and trying to get Doreen to pass the bunting out of the window. I don't know what she's doing wrong, but he just yelled, "what's wrong with you woman? A bleedin' Monkey could do it."

We aren't decorating our house! We've got some nice NHS rainbows in the window, but that's it.

Neville said, "I'm not covering our house in flags, in the same way that i'm not about to start reading The Daily Mail."

8th May - Lockdown Day 46

So today was VE day - Neville complained SO MUCH beforehand, but I think he enjoyed it in the end. It was really friendly. All the neighbours put chairs in their driveways and we all chatted to one another shouting from the street and across hedges. There were some people with BBQs in the driveway and some people with afternoon tea. A few people had decorated their houses and we all ate cakes and the adults all got drunk. The people at No.9 who never talk to anyone even came out. Derek and Doreen had Union Jack bowler hats on, and were dressed in red, white and blue. They managed to get the bunting up in the end (ALL OVER THE HOUSE) and even had 2 massive flags stuck in the front lawn. It was quite nice .. the whole day I mean .. not Derek and Doreen's decorations .. they were DEFINITELY a bit too much!

10th May - Lockdown Day 48

Right - It's Neville here .. again. Hope you are all getting on alright. I'm not so great this week. The truth is I'm pretty much bored stupid at home and I'm actually spending MORE money drinking now, than I spent when the pubs were open!

The wife seems to spend her days either waxing lyrical about gratitude for life and the beauty of nature, sunbathing for hours and drinking Gin. Or else she's crying for hours and stuffing chocolate down her neck. Her mood entirely depends on what's been on the news the day before.

She's not speaking to me right now because I asked her how come she hasn't sorted out the virus yet given the shit ton of f'ing healing crystals she's got in her collection. She's actually taken to getting guidance from Spirits beyond the grave to explain what's going on right now.

To be fair, a bunch of dead people might have a few good ideas about the whole thing .... They can't do any worse than the Government frankly.

The main news this week is that we are easing the lockdown. That seems to be the way to go ... given the UK has got the HIGHEST death rate in Europe!

*So where do I start? How about f***ing VE day?*

NOW...... LISTEN ..... I'm all for a bit of celebration, raising a glass and drinking a few beers in honour of 75 years of peace, but Derek and Doreen were really keen on the whole thing (Derek and Doreen are the nosy gits at No.16 .. hopefully they don't watch YouTube .. haha).

Anyway they put a leaflet through our door a couple of weeks back telling us to put bunting all over the house. BUNTING! Well I wasn't doing that for a start. And said they wanted us all to sit in the front garden eating tea and f'ing scones. A "Stay at Home Street Party" they called it. Now, I like a cream tea as much as the next man, but there was a printed schedule that included listening to Churchill on

TV and singing Vera Lynn songs with a bunch of people I never normally speak to!

I told Derek I'd be washing my hair that day, even though I'm bald. Jaz told me off and said it's really important to join in with local events and show a bit of community spirit.

*You know what? Community I can support ... but Vera Lynn and bleedin' Churchill .. I can't stand all these twats comparing the virus to wartime and banging on about "Dunkirk Spirit." They don't know what the f**k they are talking about unless they are about 120 - which they aren't.*

Course Jaz and Ruby said a street party sounded nice. I said I'd rather move house than take part. In the end we all stood in different bits of the street holding drinks, barbecuing sausages and shouting at one another ... turned out it was alright and everyone had a bit of a laugh, but we went indoors before half the road got pissed and forgot to social distance.

Wasn't just our street that forgot what 2 metres is .... It was absolute carnage all round the country by all accounts .. which is guaranteed to create a whole load of new cases in a couple of weeks ....

So now we have a whole bunch of new shit rules that no one really understands, but most of which seem to involve being "Alert" and controlling the virus - which is invisible and can't be controlled. If it could be controlled I'm guessing we'd have done it by now.

God knows what most of it is about .. but here's my understanding.

** Family group sports are OK - which means I could have a game of rugby with my Mum, but only if she already lives in my house - that* *would be alright if she hadn't passed away a few years ago and if she wasn't a pretty shit scrum half when she was alive.*

** I CAN'T see my Nephew, but I CAN meet a stranger in a park at a 6 foot distance - that's good - that should ensure drug deals can still continue without interruption.*

** If my Dad was my cleaner or my nanny he could pop round - unfortunately he's neither - he's in a care home that's rife with Covid-19 and suffering from dementia. To be honest if I told him he was my cleaner he'd probably believe me.*

** Estate agents are selling houses again so the only way I can see any of my mates is if I put the house up for sale and they come round for a viewing - or if they decide to become my cleaner ... or my nanny.*

That's about it I think. Apart from the fact people who can't work at home should go back to work, even though their kids can't go to school yet and if they don't have a car, they shouldn't use public transport - so even if they work miles and miles away they should walk there. Or maybe they could just play golf instead. Playing golf is fine apparently. The virus is fine with golf.

I'd probably consider taking up golf, I'm so f'ing bored - except the clubhouses are shut so I couldn't even have a beer afterwards.

So ... yeah it's a bit vague ... in fact some genius on Twitter changed the lyrics of the Matt Lucas "Thank you baked potato" song to "Thank you vague potato."

I tell you what .. when Chemical Banana start doing gigs again we will do a homage to that baked potato song.

*In fact ... we might go the whole hog and do a full on set of VE day infection songs .... The Conga, Oops upside your head, the hokey f***ing cokey, ... and for total authenticity Ring a Ring a Roses ....*

Right so .. more totally confusing rules .... So yeah ... Stay in or don't stay in. Go to work or don't go to work. But STAY ALERT, wear a mask, take up golf, play cricket with your immediate family and don't touch any surfaces .... And DO ONE Boris !

13th May - Lockdown Day 51

We are all allowed to be outdoors more now and meet people. Neville said he keeps seeing people sitting awkwardly on benches two feet apart like they are spies from the 70s. He said to Mum, "Derek was in the park talking to that bloke from the hardware shop. Opposite ends of the bench, both staring straight ahead, avoiding eye contact. I really wanted one of them to slide a newspaper to the other one and say something like 'The blue eagle is starting to nest."

I have absolutely NO idea what he is talking about, but both him and Mum found it hilarious.

Mum keeps going out and meeting Martha in the park or by the river. Things at her house have been getting worse. Mum said she locked herself in the bedroom the other day, because Terence had thrown a coffee mug against the wall in the kitchen and it smashed everywhere. Mum said, "he sounds like he's getting very violent, but she promises me he's not hurting her, or the kids, he's just angry all the time, it's just all very tense with them all stuck in the house together. Like a pressure cooker ...."

I hope Martha IS OK .. I think Mum really is worried about her. She's just gone to phone Margaret to check on her .. she's worried about her as well, but for different reasons. She lives on her own and is finding the lockdown really, really lonely because she usually has lots of visitors and goes for weekends away.

Poor Margaret, we all get on each other's nerves a bit, but at least there are three of us so no one is lonely and sometimes we even have fun together.

Anyway - I'm off to the park to meet Alice and kick a ball around … Mum has just started getting on my nerves. She is trying to write "lockdown poetry" and wanted to read me some .. OMG … I told her I'd forgotten I had plans.

18th May - Lockdown Day 56

Neville watched a programme about Covid by Charlie Brooker yesterday. He's the one that does Black Mirror - I haven't watched them, but they are supposed to be good. Mum and Neville both said it was really, really funny, but ever since Charlie Brooker said Matt Hancock looks like "your sister's first boyfriend with a car," Neville hasn't stopped giggling about it.

Everyone is being sarcastic about the new 3 word slogan - Stay Alert - Control the Virus - Save Lives. People keep making jokes about staying alert. Mum said when she was small they used to say, "stay alert, the world needs lerts."

Ed Gamble was funny on Twitter he said, "Guys remember to stay alert. I was just out for a walk and saw a piece of virus coming towards me, but because I was being alert I managed to dive out of the way."

They are saying they might open the schools again on 1st of June. I really hope they don't. I actually like studying at home. Mum says it's too soon and it won't happen.

20th May - Lockdown Day 58

Ollie seems to have caused a bit of a drama .... He's posted all his lockdown achievements online in a so-called "motivational" post. Neville is definitely not impressed (or motivated).

Mum said lots of people with big audiences on social media post these as inspiration for their followers .... I didn't think it sounds very inspirational, it just sounded like a big list of showing off to me.

I can't remember exactly but it was something like ... since the start of lockdown I've decreased my body fat by whatever, increased my muscle mass by whatever, improved my 10k speed, increased the amount I can lift by, like, loads. Set up a new business, started writing a book, started a YouTube Channel, hit millions of subscribers, started a podcast, was a guest on 10 other people's podcasts and advised other fitness pros how to navigate the lockdown and profit from it. . blah blah blah.

It ended with "Over to you guys ... what have you done?"

LOADS of people have commented, most of them were fitness people saying how successfully they had "pivoted" to online classes or just congratulating Olllie saying stuff like "you're an absolute legend mate."

One nurse said, "Well I've been too busy saving lives in the ICU to find time to become an online legend you bellend ... back over to you."

Neville wrote, "I've eaten thousands of pounds worth of cheese and made very good friends with one of our house plants."

21st May - Lockdown Day 59

Mum decided it would be nice to go and see Grandma and Grandpa and sit in the garden with them. She called Grandma to say would it be OK if we drove over tomorrow. Grandma said, “well I’ve got online pilates at 10 and we do a lunchtime Zoom with our old friends at 12.”

I heard Mum say to Neville, “unbelievable - I haven’t seen them since February, and they are literally confined to the house aside from a daily walk, and they are still too busy to see us!”

In the end Mum decided we’d get there about 2 after their Zoom lunch, stay for a couple of hours to chat and then come home again.

22nd May - Lockdown Day 60

McDonalds opened up a few of their drive throughs across the country today. The queues were CRAZY. Of course we didn’t go, cos Mum hates it [eyeroll], but even I don’t want one badly enough to sit in a massive queue for ages.

So, as planned, we went to Grandmas instead. For the first time since February - that’s the longest I haven’t seen them since I was BORN.

We took our own tea in a flask, and our own plates and we took scones and jam and cream for us and a bag for them (so we could all have stuff together). Because it was lovely and warm we sat in the garden on one side and they sat on the other and we all had scones and tea together. It was better than talking through the patio door which was what Uncle Dave had to do when it was cold, so I’m glad it was a nice day. It was really lovely and so much nicer seeing them like .. in the flesh .. and not on Zoom.

I really wanted to give them a hug and I couldn’t. That was the really weird bit.

At one point Grandpa was walking back from the kitchen with more tea, and I was heading to the toilet, and I walked a bit too near to him - he sort of jumped sideways and shouted "urgghhghhhhghgh" really loudly as if something disgusting had touched him. I just sort of forgot about keeping my distance.

We were only out for a few hours, but the dog went MENTAL when we got back. She whizzed around like an absolute LOONEY and knocked a pot plant over with her tail. It's the first time the house has been empty for MONTHS .. she probably thought we'd abandoned her forever.

25th May - Lockdown Day 63

Boris said that people can go to beaches now and have picnics as long as they all do social distancing. All the other Countries that have loosened their lockdowns say everyone has to wear masks in shops AND in the streets, but there aren't any mask rules here. Except in supermarkets. It's really hot weather so all that has happened is that loads and loads of people are going to the beaches. The pictures on the news and on the front of the papers show the beaches are ABSOLUTELY packed!

Me and Em went and met in the park which was really nice - we got some sandwiches and sat apart chatting.

In America, a man called George Floyd was killed by a policeman - they arrested him and one of them held him down by kneeling on his NECK … until he DIED!!! People videoed it and tried to stop them. It was absolutely horrible.

26th May - Lockdown Day 64

Evening .. Neville here. Phew .. bit of a week .. even by 2020 standards. It's all kicking off a bit to be honest.

There's loads of crap going on in the UK because Boris's Special Advisor Cummings has broken the lockdown rules. We all get told to stay at home and isolate and this twat thinks it's fine to drive halfway across the country with symptoms to stay at his parent's house. He said he was too ill to look after his son so had to drive there. Later on he went on a little day out with his wife to somewhere called Barnard Castle.

Boris just defended him and said he had "acted responsibly, legally and with integrity," because he drove 260 miles to isolate and that "any parent would frankly understand what he did."

There was A LOT of fuss in the media - the old "one rule for them and one for us." So Downing Street set up a SPECIAL press conference so Cummings could defend himself.

What a shitshow that was! The arrogant git sat there and came out with a really complicated explanation for why he went there (too ill to cope with his son) and why he went on a day out to a castle (said he couldn't see properly and thought he'd go driving to "test his eyesight"). Biggest load of bollocks I've ever heard .... Why couldn't he just say that he shouldn't have broken the rules and he was sorry?? .. Instead it's just LIES. More and more lies.

Seriously, these politicians must think we are total MUGS!

Oh and if things are messed up here .. it's nothing on America! ... There are tons of protests starting up over there - all about the police murdering that man, George Floyd. The Black Lives Matter movement are organising protests even though people are NOT supposed to gather in groups and the police are wading it trying to break up the protests .. it's getting really violent. Ellie's been on WhatsApp today saying it looks like it could all really escalate.

So lots of anger about a few different things at the moment ...

So yeah ... Cummings can DO ONE .. the lying git, Boris can DO ONE for not sacking him and those police that committed actual MURDER can definitely DO ONE.

'Til next time folks ... who knows what the next episode will bring?

28th May - Lockdown Day 66

Tonight is the last time clapping for the NHS. The lady whose idea it was said that today was week 10 and that it was a good time to stop. It started out really well, but after a while not everyone bothered. I was in the bath one week, because I forgot and another time Neville ran out in his dressing gown, because he got a message on the neighbourhood WhatsApp from Derek asking why he wasn't out on the doorstep. He was on his Xbox at the time.

Tonight though Mum was cheering a bit too loudly to be honest (embarrassing). She said it was because it's the "very last clap for carers" ... more like it was because she'd spent the whole afternoon drinking with Bridget, Jane and Dibbie .. all spread out in Bridget's garden.

She said it was lovely, but they kept having to remember not to hug and to stand and shout at one another from a couple of metres distance.

Oh and everyone keeps making jokes about going for long drives to test their eyesight. I was a bit confused, but Neville said, "just more Government lies Ruby don't worry."

31st May - Lockdown Day 69

It's the Bank Holiday weekend. The beaches are packed, the Black Lives Matter protests are getting bigger in America and smaller ones are starting up here in the UK as well. Ellie is really passionate about it in the family WhatsApp and Uncle John keeps posting stuff saying "All Lives Matter," because he knows it will really wind her up and he enjoys that. It's like when he wears his Trump merchandise on FaceTime. Works every time.

I wish we had been to the beach, but the nearest one is like nearly 3 hours away and people aren't really supposed to be driving to places if they don't need to, and you can't stay overnight so it's a long way to go in a day. Mum tried to convince us that a nice BBQ in the garden would cheer us all up. We literally have a nice BBQ in the garden every few days .. I NEVER thought I'd get sick of eating burgers, but right now it's looking that that totally might happen.

2nd June - Lockdown Day 71

Speaking of burgers, 168 more McDonalds opened today - the police had to shut roads and redirect the traffic in some places because there were 2 HOUR QUEUES. 2 HOURS .. seriously .. you'd have to be really keen to wait that long for a happy meal.

Grandpa said in the WhatsApp group that he'd never heard such nonsense in all his life. Ella said, "Honestly Grandpa, this is like THE BEST NEWS EVER .. just gotta wait for Nandos now. Totally Sic"

And Grandpa replied, "Yes .. exactly, It WILL make you sick young lady, you need to eat proper food."

5th June - Lockdown Day 74

Mum is moaning about her "lockdown weight" all the time and was ATTEMPTING to do one of Ollie's HiiT workouts earlier. I walked past her lying on the floor of the lounge, flailing about, and looking like a heart attack about to happen. Neville said, "Blimey, she looks like that fish in Finding Nemo, when he jumps out of the tank and is lying on the dentist's tray gasping for breath."

She got angry with the pair of us and said, "Well you try doing it." So I did - it wasn't that hard - just not my kind of thing. Neville tried too, but only managed about 3 minutes before claiming his asthma was playing up a bit due to the high pollen count this year. He said, "Never mind Covid-19 … Hayfever-20 will be the death of me at this rate."

I told Tom about Ollie's workouts .. it's more his kind of thing than mine. He likes fitness stuff. He's a really good footballer.

Neville is acting more and more weird. Mum says he's reached something called "peak lockdown," because he's bought a label maker and is going around the house labelling EVERYTHING. He says he got it so he could organise the pantry and label all the spice jars, but now I have a sign that says "urination station" on my toilet, "squirty thing" on my tap and my fan says "Windy McWindface."

He really needs his job back.

Speaking of "peak lockdown" Mum just showed me Martha's latest post on Facebook .. it's a line of about 9 empty shot glasses. The caption said, "I'm playing a new drinking game. Anyone want to join me? You just have to drink a shot EVERY time your husband is a condescending PRICK. I've done this many shots already and it's only 11.00am."

Then Mum disappeared pretty quickly to take Martha out for a walk.

7th June - Lockdown Day 76

More stuff is kicking off in the UK about Black Lives Matter .. there are people protesting in big groups that say they are social distancing, but the papers are printing pictures that make it look like they aren't. So there's lots of angry people out there shouting about rules. Mum said it's the camera lenses, and that, from certain angles, you can make people look really squashed together when they are actually spread out quite safely. She said the media are probably doing it to cause trouble.

There was massive "hoo ha" (Grandma's word) and "palava" (Grandpa's word), this weekend, because a bunch of protesters in Bristol pulled down the statue of a famous slave trader and chucked it in the sea. As usual things got really heated in the WhatsApp with Auntie Ellie going on and on about how slave traders shouldn't have monuments and they should all be taken down, and Grandpa saying that no one supports slavery, but you can't just tear down statues and rewrite history.

I wasn't really interested so I didn't join in. I tried to watch this really scary thing on Netflix called The Haunting of Hill House … but it was a bit too creepy so I rewatched a whole load of old episodes of Queer Eye instead.

I made some chocolate chip cookies earlier for something to do. They are SO nice. It reminded me a bit of the start of lockdown when we were all cheerful and we did home baking and played board games. Well if I'm honest we played like ONE game of monopoly and me and Neville did Battleships one evening, but to be honest that was about it.

Mum and Neville are taking part in a Zoom "Desert Island Discs" Birthday Party - they are dressed in stupid outfits and playing songs from Spotify very loudly. I grabbed the tin with all the homemade cookies in and went off to my room. They were still REALLY loud even with the door shut and my music on. I really need better earphones to drown the pair of them out …

10th June - Lockdown Day 79

YASSSSS !!!!!! Primark is open again.

I literally can't wait to go shopping …

11th June - Lockdown Day 80

Mum has refused to take me shopping

13th June .. It's not really like proper lockdown, so I'm not counting any more!

There's a new thing called a "support bubble." Mum said it's fabulous for people like Margaret that live alone because they can now visit people in their support bubble and stay overnight so they get to be with other people and not alone anymore. I think that sounds really nice.

Also I want to change my room .. I am SOOOO sick of it. My desk finally turned up so I can get rid of the picnic table I've been doing all my school work on. Mum and Neville have agreed to get me a new bed and wardrobe and shelves and stuff.

14th June

This statue thing seems to have gone a bit mad … why are people so bothered about statues???

Grandpa said there were about 100 people arrested in London yesterday (well .. he actually called them "thugs" and "herberts" not people). They were supposedly protecting statues in case people wanted to damage them, but it all got pretty nasty between them and the Black Lives Matter protesters.

One man got arrested for having a wee on the memorial of a policeman who'd been killed by a terrorist. He said him and his mates from football were in London protecting the statues. Neville said most of those arrested were "far-right racists," but he didn't think the man had intended to be disrespectful to the policeman's memorial. He said, "paper says the bloke had had 16 pints with his mates, so he was probably desperate for a piss. Can't imagine that amount of build-up .. blimey."

Also seemed like the man didn't really know which statues they'd come to protect in the first place. Maybe him and his mates just fancied a day out ? I know I'd like a day out … I am soooooooooo sick of staring at the same 4 walls in my bedroom, or the lounge or whatever … I know we aren't really locked down so much now, but I still can't do sleepovers or anything .. and me and Tom really, REALLY want to meet up. Like in REAL LIFE. It's so weird that we've just talked on a screen.

Margaret called to say her friend who lives a few hours away is on her way to spend a couple of days with her … she's really excited. They both live alone so have had a really, really hard time, and been really lonely over the lockdown. They are being each other's support bubble.

That's really nice.

Later on Margaret WhatsApped Mum to say they spent about 20 minutes hugging and crying when her friend arrived .. and then drank lots. Sounds about right for Mum's friends. It must have been really hard not having anyone to be with or hug for 3 whole months!

16th June

OMG .. MASSIVE MASSIVE MASSIVE DRAMA !!!!

Terence Appleby CAME OUT yesterday! He's left Martha for his friend Trevor.

Mum said he's in Trevor's support bubble, because Trevor lives alone so he's gone to live with him. Like permanently. She reckons it turns out Terence has known he was gay for ages, but had been putting off doing anything about it because the children are still so young.

It was Philip Schofield coming out that did it, made him decide it was time to tell Martha and talk about them separating, but then suddenly we were in lockdown and he couldn't leave the house for 3 months. Them being forced to spend all that time together, with no escape for work or anything, was the end of it or "the nail in the coffin" as Mum put it.

Martha and Mum have been on FaceTime together for literally hours going on and on and on about it. I don't know why they have to analyse everything so much.

Martha : To be honest Jaz, I was really upset to start with and then I realised I wasn't really that surprised. It kind of makes sense looking back on everything now. He stopped noticing me a while back - like if I had lost weight or had my hair done. Also kind of explains why the counselling was a bit of a disaster and he moved into the spare room. I mean it was obvious he wasn't attracted to ME anymore, I just thought he was having an affair with another woman. How funny is that? How did I not realise? He spent a ridiculous amount of time with Trevor. I'm an idiot !! Anyway he's apologised for being so aggressive all the time. He said lockdown just finished him off.

Neville : Well thank God for that Martha ... genuinely … I was a bit worried he might have been beating you up or something. Good to know he's just an angry poof.

Mum: NEVILLE !! Don't use words like that.

Martha: It's fine Jaz. You aren't the only one Neville. To be honest a few people have contacted me privately to check that I was OK. Everyone was worried when I finally started to be honest about how unhappy I've been and stopped pretending to be the perfect wife.

Mum : At least it was just bad moods and nothing else. God it's frightening though, all these people trapped in abusive relationships in lockdown .. with no break from it. Absolutely awful.

Martha : Horrendous - I'm fortunate it was just lockdown stress. You know, I thought for SO long that there was something wrong with me .. I was always trying to do everything perfectly. Then it turns out he's always fancied men. Trevor's welcome to him.

Yeah so that was that!

The biggest bit of gossip in the whole lockdown. Bit of excitement at least. Makes a change !

Hope the kids are OK with it. Must be a bit weird for them, but they'll probably all be happier once they get used to everything.

20th June

Mum and Neville went to IKEA to get me a new bed and some other stuff for my room. They were gone for HOURS and drank lots of wine when they got home. They actually hate IKEA normally, but because of Covid, it was EVEN worse. They had to queue for a really long time in the carpark, through those roped sections like they have at passport control in the airport. They were only letting people in 2 at a time, and you had to wait for 2 people to come out for that to happen.

Neville said, "like a nightclub, except even more sh*t." He also said their hand sanitiser smelt like neat Tequila and gave him flashbacks to being very ill when he was younger.

Mum is really unhappy right now. When I asked her what the matter was, she said, "I was supposed to be flying to Malaga yesterday Ruby. I should be in the hills, in a remote bit of Andalucia, decompressing on a fabulous yoga retreat. Instead NONE of my clothes fit and I spent the afternoon in bloody IKEA."

21st June

Today was Father's Day and we met the whole family together in Grandma and Grandpa's garden, it was also Ella's Birthday a couple of days ago so it was a double celebration - we had a BBQ, but everyone brought their own drinks and plates and glasses. There were birthday presents and Father's Day presents. We were only allowed INSIDE the house to use the toilet. There was lots of hand sanitiser outside the bathroom door, but Grandma and Grandpa were still worried about germs and told people not to touch anything unnecessarily, which included the lock on the bathroom door. Instead Grandpa put a big sign on the door that said, "Please open and close the door using your foot and sing whilst you are doing your business, so we all know when the bathroom is occupied."

They are VERY weird sometimes.

They'd set up the garden a bit like one you'd have at a pub, so each family had their own separate table and we all yelled across the lawn at each other. Coco and Felix kept running over to people and getting a bit too near so we had to send them away again. They are actually really good at following the rules considering how little they are.

Everyone social distanced really well until Ella got everyone - including Grandpa - to get up to learn a TikTok dance. By the end we were all standing in one big group, all really close together, so she could fit us all on the video properly. Grandpa got the hang of it pretty well to be honest and Ella told him he was a "legend' and "well good at learning a dance."

Neville and Uncle Dave were kind of in the "awkward dad dancing" category and Mum just looked like she was doing her own dance to a completely different song. Neville said it looked the sort of "hippy interpretive dance" you'd see members of a commune do. That annoyed her.

It was really, really lovely to see everyone though. The not hugging thing was still so weird, but it was SUCH a nice day.

22nd June

My room looks great - I've got new furniture and my new bed is smaller so I have waaay more room. EVERYTHING came in a flat pack so Neville drank 8 beers and put A LOT of money in the swearing jar whilst he put it together.

23rd June

OMG. Alice's family have ALL got Coronavirus. They've been ill for a few days now. They all have completely different symptoms to each other. Alice just had a temperature and a headache for a couple of days, her Dad just felt tired and lost his sense of smell and taste. Her little brother just seemed totally normal - and kept complaining because no one had the energy to play with him. But her Mum has felt really, really ill - she's taking lots of painkillers, has a really nasty cough and very high temperature. She's aching and feels sick too. It's really horrid.

Mum's been round and left food parcels on the doorstep and she's been walking their dog for them. They have to stay indoors and can't see anyone at all. She's being really obsessive about scrubbing her hands every time she gets back from a dog walk.

27th June

Neville is STILL having a go at making Sourdough bread. To be honest I'm quite impressed that he is still even trying .. he's binned SO MANY of them. Em came over yesterday and upset him by saying, "Oh are you making Sourdough Neville? My dad's making it all the time as well - it's really yummy toasted. He says it's really easy once you get the hang of it."

Neville looked annoyed and stomped off to the shed.

Me and Em spent about 3 hours doing make up and making a bunch of TikTok videos.

29th June

*Neville here .. so the pubs are going to be opening again on Saturday. Now don't get me wrong I f***ing LOVE going to the pub, my beer shed's been keeping me a bit sane through this, but getting back to the actual pub will be ABSOLUTELY brilliant.*

But even I'm thinking ... is it a good idea? We've got about 45,000 people that have died, the NHS staff and care staff are knackered, loads of people on furlough have lost their jobs, the arts are screwed, events are screwed and the economy is going down the toilet and Boris is out there going "Never mind the killer virus, never mind that we still don't have a decent track and trace system, it's alright everyone because we can all go out and get pissed again!!" (well he didn't use those words, but you get the point).

So I STILL can't go and see my Dad, but I can go to Wetherspoons with a bunch of people I don't know!

*And holidays .. holidays are back on .. you can go and stay somewhere self-catering or hotels if they are open with covid measures. They are telling everyone to get booking holidays abroad by offering massive discounts - we still don't have tests at airports so we'll be importing the virus all over again .. but God forbid Susan from f***ing Preston misses her annual trip to Benidorm just because there's a pandemic!*

I'd like to be going on holiday myself, but I don't know when furlough ends or if they are even letting us take any holiday time when we get back. I suppose that's fair enough ... but still .. smug gits that share holiday photos can just Do One!

2nd July - Officially day 100 of Lockdown

Today is the 100th official day of Lockdown … not that we are really locked down anymore because we can go away for weekends and meet in people's gardens. To quote Neville "it stopped being a proper lockdown when a bunch of thick twats swarmed the beaches."

Mum says it was never a proper lockdown anyway .. not like they did in places like New Zealand - they seem to have done everything brilliantly and hardly anyone died.

It was quite nice some days .. but we are all pretty bored of everything to be honest. No one really knows what day it is since we stopped clapping for the NHS, unless it's bin day. We just get up whenever, sometimes ALL of us wear PJs all day. There are days Mum and Neville are lying on sofas in different rooms for the WHOLE DAY. Mum is kind of doing a bit of work, but Neville is STILL on furlough so he just plays video games and spends hours in his beer shed.

They don't even sunbathe any more. We hardly ever go for a family walk. Mum occasionally walks to the shops (for wine) and Neville walks the dog as often as possible to get out of the house. There was lots of talk of painting and new hobbies and getting fit and growing vegetables.

By the way .. we literally grew NO vegetables. Mum made Neville dig a vegetable patch at the end of the garden, but they never planted anything so now there's just a patch of pointless ground next to the shed! It looks a right state.

I'm LITERALLY the only one who is actually working hard !!!!

And every conversation we have is about food. Seriously .. like EVERY. SINGLE. ONE.

OMG.

So since it's the official 100th day, Mum and Neville are both showing off about the fact they have an unbroken record of 100 solid days of drinking. Mum was going on about how she should get some sort of medal for it … like the ones people get at Alcoholics Anonymous to count the days. Only in reverse. It's like the total OPPOSITE of 100 days sober. They don't even get hangovers anymore .. it must be because they actually don't stop drinking. I saw Neville open a beer with his scrambled eggs the other morning and say "f**k it."

Mum is also doing no exercise. She was going for runs quite often before all this because she did the Couch to 5K programme and joined a running group. She's literally doing that in reverse now too. She could trademark the 5k to Couch programme. She barely gets off the couch. She's even stopped doing her drunken Zoom girls' nights because everyone is bored and you can now meet a couple of friends in someone's garden instead.

Actually I lied when I said she only leaves the house to buy wine. She's got drunk 3 times in people's gardens in the last few weeks. And she does actually go to the Post Office a lot. She is constantly returning all the clothes she bought online because she's too FAT for any of them…nearly all the shops are actually open now, so she could just try stuff on now. I want to go to Primark and New Look, but she's still refusing to take me because of how long the queues are. I told her it's probably like 20 minutes, so it's the same as going to Tescos for wine, but she wouldn't give in. It's not like I want her to sit at a drive through McDonald's for 2 hours like people were doing when they first opened.

I'm counting the days until I can go shopping again - I don't even want her to come with me - I said she could just give me a load of money and drop me and Em off while she sleeps in the car!! But she says she can't be bothered to leave the house.

OMG … So lazy.

And talking of counting the days .. Neville just goes on and on about how brilliant it will be when the pub opens. He's got one of those charts on the wall (like in prison films) with four vertical lines and one diagonal line across them. Seriously .. Sad.

Anyway … here's MY list of the most annoying things about lockdown

* Mum asking me what I want for dinner about 4 or 5 times a day
* Neville asking me if Mum's asked me about dinner yet - also about 4 or 5 times a day
* Mum saying "the new normal" all the time
* Neville saying "unprecedented" all the time
* Mum banging on about failing to plant any vegetables
* Neville banging on about failing to bake any Sourdough
* Mum saying "it can't be bin day again, we only just put the bins out.. where are the days going?"
* Neville saying "I only know what day it is because I just put the bins out"
* Mum banging on about the sound of birdsong getting quieter because of the traffic coming back
* Neville telling Mum to stop banging on about bird noise
* Mum saying how desperate she is for the hairdressers to open
* Neville saying how desperate he is for the pub to open
* Mum moaning about how much weight she's put on eating so much food
* Neville moaning about how much money we are spending on all the food.

Mum just paused from her drinking for a few seconds to shout the word "UNIFORM !!!!" at me … it's been a really, really long time since she did that … but I am actually going to school tomorrow for like 4 whole hours … SO ANNOYING .. it'll take me almost that long to put my makeup on …..

3rd July

My alarm went off at 7 o'clock …. SERIOUSLY 7 o'clock !!!!

I haven't woken up at 7 in the morning for like months … it was HORRIBLE. I didn't get to lie around in bed, or decide whether to get dressed. I had to get up and do my hair and make up and everything .. just to spend 4 hours at school .. wearing a mask. It's stupid !!

Our form teacher was really happy to see us .. that's a bit sad. I haven't missed him so I have no idea why he's missed us. The boys' hair is kind of back to normal, most of their hair is long and untidy because the hairdressers don't officially open until tomorrow. Jake decided to keep his skinhead as it suits him so much.

So Boris has been calling tomorrow "Super Saturday" and all the papers picked up on it .. just because the pubs are opening and it's the first time in 3 months people can "drink a pint in a pub." I seriously don't get it .. Neville's drunk HUNDREDS of pints .. it's not like he's missed out. He was trying to explain why it's different to actually be the pub for a pint, but I lost interest half way through and walked out of the room.

The pubs are opening at 6am! Who would go to the pub THAT early? Neville said, "6am? That's completely ridiculous. I won't be going until at least 9am."

Mum said it's completely disrespectful for the Country to be celebrating the re-opening of the pubs when so many people have died.

4th July - Super Saturday

My phone pinged pretty early this morning .. it was Ella, in the family WhatsApp.

Ella: YES !!! 'Spoons is open again … it's ON! Getting smashed today."

Grandma: You be careful Ella. This virus is still out there, make sure you social distance and don't touch any surfaces in there.

Uncle Dave: The state of those places, she'll get plenty of other diseases in there, never mind the 'Rona.

I'm REALLY, REALLY nervous. I'm meeting Tom today .. me and Em are meeting him and some of his mates over where he lives. Neville was going to give me a lift, but he's already left for the pub. Mum said she'll do it. I told her she can drop me off on the corner before we get to his house. I seriously don't want her to actually SPEAK to him. She keeps saying, "will it be weird to meet him in the flesh?" It's making me EVEN MORE nervous. Also, I wish she'd stop saying FLESH!

I've done all my hair and make up, which is fine, but seriously can't decide what to wear .. I've changed like 5 times. And I've got a spot. Mum says she can't see it but it's like MASSIVE. TOTAL nightmare.

5th July

Yesterday was so cool. Tom is lovely. And tall. And fit. He's actually really tall - definitely next to me - he doesn't look that tall on FaceTime. Neville said, "that's because he's always sitting down, you burke." That's not what I meant.

Then he said, "didn't you warn him that you're a midget." He's sooo not funny.

I knew Mum would be embarrassing when she came to get me - I told her to text me when she was outside and NOT come anywhere near the front door. She actually did what I said for once.

6th July

The hairdressers are OPEN again! I can't wait to get my hair done dark PROPERLY. It's not ginger anymore, but having the hairdresser do it will be so cool. Mind you I'm still Ron Weasley in everyone's phones.

Me and Mum are going together - we can have a double appointment because we are in a bubble - the hairdressers can't fit as many people in because of all the cleaning in between.

Mum's hair has turned into a total haystack because it's thick and curly. She keeps going on about the roots. The roots are the least of the problem. I told her they don't really show because she's got loads of grey hair, it just needs a cut.

That made her burst into tears. She does that a lot lately. Neville says her menopause is getting worse. I think it's because she hasn't been away anywhere. She's always liked going away by herself to her retreat things and meditation things and she was really, really upset she couldn't go to Spain.

11 July

My new hair looks amazing!! It's a gorgeous brown and has some lowlights .. so nice. Mum's looks better too - the hairdresser chopped loads off and did a fringe. I like it, but Grandpa managed to really upset her because he told her she looked like someone from the band The Sweet. Neville laughed his head off and said they were a glam rock band from the 70s. I looked them up. Not only did they have terrible hair, but they are all men. I told Grandpa that Mum was upset so he sent a text to say, "your haircut does make you look younger though."

So Neville said, "there you are Jaz, at least you look like a YOUNG male 70s glam rock artist."

14th July

New rule was announced today. ANOTHER ONE. This time about wearing masks in all shops. It's going to be mandatory. I didn't know what that meant. Mum said it means you HAVE to wear them, like it's not a choice. It's actually the law. Coco most likely knows the word "mandatory," it's probably on her special words flip-chart.

So they said that we HAVE to do it, but that we don't have to do it until the 24th July … that's a bit weird .. I don't really get that. Mum says they should have said this at the START of the pandemic and not left it until we are coming out of lockdown. It's like they don't have a clue what they are actually doing …

17th July

I had another 4 whole hours in school this morning. All the boys are really distracting in class. I'd totally forgotten how annoying they are - even when we are in really small groups. I actually prefer working at home doing Google Classroom - I can concentrate much easier and get everything done quicker.

19th July

We went to visit Uncle Dave and Auntie Sally to sit in their garden for a BBQ yesterday. That was really nice. The weather is so nice - it's really, really sunny. I actually got a bit sunburned.

It was actually a double BBQ weekend - Mum and Neville have gone to The Turbot's house (she's another one of Mum's friend's with a weird nickname). I didn't want to go, so me and the dog stayed home. Margaret is visiting for a couple of days. She seems to have loads of people in her bubble now. Mum said, "well if people are getting on planes and going off on holiday then Margaret can stay at a friend's house for a couple of nights. All these stupid rules that contradict each other. There'll be more mental health issues than Covid deaths by the time this is finished."

She showed me some photos when they got home - mostly all of them sat close together. Arms round one another … so much for social distance. I think everyone's a bit sick of it all now to be honest and wants a cuddle now and then.

20th July

Seriously, every SINGLE thing that anyone says they've done they now add "socially distanced of course" on the end. And it's on instagram photos and facebook posts. I JUST heard Mum on the phone to Martha saying, "we had SUCH a wonderful day yesterday. It really does feel different actually being near people and not seeing faces on Zoom .. no, oh yes … and the food was great. A BBQ .. socially distanced of course."

Literally every photo she took yesterday shows people hugging.

23rd July

Trump did some weird test thing, where he had to remember a bunch of words. He's all over the news saying, "person, woman, man, camera, TV" over and over and over. Mum said he's trying to make out he's a genius. He said, "they said nobody gets it in order, it's actually not that easy. But for me it was easy."

Neville said, "the man's an idiot. Didn't anyone tell him it was a dementia test, my Dad did something similar."

Tomorrow is my last 4 hours in school then it's the summer holidays. Loads of people are going away, but we haven't booked anything in case we just had to cancel it again. I'm going to be SOOOO bored. Mum just keeps going on about next year. What if next year is worse than this year? At least we'd have a nice holiday to look back on.

Still, Tom isn't going away either so at least we can hang out. I am going to watch him play football on Saturday.

24th July

It's the end of year 10. So weird. We weren't at school for literally half of it !

The mask rules started today. Mum was online earlier, ordering all kinds of pretty ones for us both from different places and she's got some from local people that are sewing them for charity. She said to Neville, "I've ordered a load of masks for me and Ruby."

And he said, "Oh, so Neville can just die then can he?"

25th July

So it's the first day of the Summer Holidays. This literally means NOTHING except we don't have to sign into Google Classroom.

Every day still just feels like it's the same. Well except that me and Em watched Tom play footie today. More people are out and about everywhere and the roads are busy again, but it just doesn't really feel NORMAL. Even though people keep talking about the "New Normal" ALL THE TIME. That's annoying.

Em REALLY likes Tom's friend Jack. He's cute. And he's funny. They totally got beaten though. Like 8-2. I felt a bit bad for them. Then I had pizza at his house. His Mum and Dad are really nice.

Mum got really upset when I said that. She said, "Oh OK, so you can go and have a nice chat with his parents, but me and Neville aren't even allowed to look in his direction, let alone say hello to him."

Bit of an exaggeration.

I told her that's because HIS Mum and Dad are NORMAL. Now she's not speaking to me and has been having a bath for about an hour. So annoying. I need to wash my hair.

27th July

Now that the pubs are open, the Government is trying to get EVEN MORE people to go in them .. even though being in places with other people is supposed to be a bad idea. So they've got a new scheme out (with a new slogan of course!) Eat Out to Help Out - it's a thing offering discounts for families to go to restaurants and stuff through the whole of August.

Neville said it will "encourage a load of breeding grounds for the plague" .. he keeps calling it that, it's so annoying .. this is nothing like the plague, that's one of the few things from history I remember .. even when I was little we did loads of stuff about that. And the Great Fire of London. And Henry the Eighth.

29th July

Right ... Mask twats!!!

We've got the law now - MANDATORY masks in ALL the shops and ALL public transport unless you've got a MEDICAL exemption.

So what have we got ???

The "alone in the car' Covidiots. Why would you drive along, in your own car, with no passengers and no windows open, wearing a mask ? I get if you are a taxi driver, with actual passengers. But if it's your own kids? What's the point? I don't suppose you are wearing a mask all day in your own home are you? Maybe you are! Idiots.

Then there's the "what about my rights?" Covidiots. The "we are all being controlled" lot. They think they can do exactly what they want and just refuse to wear a mask. Well I suggest the NHS refuse to treat them. And that we refuse to give them vaccines too, when the time comes. Mind you .. this lot won't even want the vaccines .. given the whole "Bill Gates wants to inject toxins into us and turn us into cyborgs" thing. These are also the "I won't download the app, no one is allowed to know my every move" Covidiots. Same people that carry a mobile phone that literally knows your every move.

The "chin only" Covidiots, you've seen them. The ones that wear the mask round their chin and not over their mouth.

The "nose out" Covidiots - these ones DO actually manage to wear the mask over their mouth, but leave their nose fully exposed.

I mean seriously ? How hard is it to wear a simple mask on your face. We are not talking full PPE here, like they wear in the ICU for 12 hours straight. It's a bit of material over your mouth and nose.

If you haven't got the common sense to put a mask on properly, or you are refusing on principle - just DO ONE!

It doesn't bloody help when Boris's bleedin' Dad is photographed in a shop not wearing one, along with tons of idiot MPs on trains without masks. This is the same Boris's Dad that flew off to Greece in the lockdown remember. Same old, same old. One rule for the plebs, different rule for them lot.

So ALL the mask Covidiots can Do One.
Stanley Johnson can Do One too - along with his scruffy bloody son.

1st August

So the government's Eat Out to Help Out thing has started and everywhere is really, really busy. It's mad. Neville says that just 3 days ago they were saying that, as a Nation, we are OBESE and need to be careful how much we eat in the fight against Covid. Then they literally give us money off if we go out and eat loads of food! You really couldn't make this stuff up.

4th August

Mum and The Turbot are away together. They've gone on a road trip to stay with Margaret. Me and Mum had tickets to see "Everyone's talking about Jamie," tonight, I was really looking forward to it, but all the theatres are shut and no one knows when they can open again. And I don't know when the Billie Eilish tour is going to be happening now - I should have been seeing that at The O2 a few nights ago as well. I don't see why people can sit in planes all squashed in to go on holiday, but they can't sit in a theatre or at a concert all squashed in. People could wear masks for both? Makes absolutely no sense to me.

Yeah so Mum will most likely spend 3 days drinking gin and talking rubbish. That's the usual way it goes.

Meanwhile me and Neville went to Uncle Dave and Auntie Sally's for a little get-together for Felix's birthday. He's 3 now. The big news is that Auntie Sophie and Uncle Marc are moving out of London and have found a lovely house not far from Uncle Dave's house. The kids don't know yet because it's not final until the paperwork is all done and people have signed these contract things you have to do when you buy a house. But Grandpa kept putting his foot in it and saying things about new houses and stuff like "when you start your new school Coco." Auntie Sophie kept telling him off. Luckily Coco and Felix were having a water fight with the garden hose, so they weren't taking much notice of him.

Ella was really fed up because all the music festivals are cancelled. She was supposed to go to Latitude in July and Reading at the end of the month. Grandma said at least she didn't have a holiday with friends that she was missing out on, like when 6 of them went to Malia last year.

She said "yeah, I decided I'd just do festival weekends this year Grandma. Malia was well expensive! So I thought I'd see some bands and then go somewhere hot with Mum and Dad. That way they could like pay for everything yeah? It's, like, seriously a lot of money when you are drinking like ALL day and ALL night for 2 weeks."

Grandma said, "well you don't have to do that, do you Ella? You could go and see the sights. Maybe go to a museum?"

Ella replied, "you are well funny Grandma .. can you imagine?"

Grandpa muttered, "Philistine," whatever that is.

7th August

Mum's back and planning her next weekend away. She hasn't stopped going on and on and on about how nice a "change of scene" was. Alright for her. Me and Neville haven't been anywhere. Maybe we'd like a change of scene too. But it's Jane and Bridget's 50th Birthdays so they are planning something for that now that going on holidays is OK.

Boris is rattling on about the Nation getting "back to work." But the Scientists say that the test and trace has to be working properly so we don't get a "Second Wave." That's a thing with viruses apparently. And they are worse in Winter. We haven't really got rid of it so it might come back again. Neville is waiting to hear about when he has to come off of furlough - I think he's had enough now. Lots of his friends at work have been made redundant, but they seem to want him to stay. I don't know what he does at work, but it sounds like whatever it is it's actually USEFUL.

Hard to believe really.

10th August

Neville's finally been able to go and see his Dad in person. His Dad is doing OK really, which is pretty amazing considering everything that's gone on and how much worse this is for old people. The staff let them sit in the garden as much as possible because the weather's so nice. So they had some tea and cakes in the sun and had a really good chat, despite his Dad thinking Neville was one of the staff. He went along with it because it was really nice to actually spend time with his Dad and it didn't really matter that he thought he was someone else.

I think it's really sad, but Neville said he's got used to it. I know it still upsets him though .. whatever he says.

He went straight to the pub when he got back.

When he got back later he said the pub was "rammed" because of Eat Out to Help Out. Even though it's meant to be table service only, he said people are still going to the bar. Then they are seeing friends across the room and going to say hi, and moving chairs around and sitting at the wrong tables or grabbing tables before they've been cleaned properly. Then there are people getting half way across the room to go to the toilet and then realising they've forgotten their mask, so they have to go back again. Sounds a bit mad. He said all the staff look really stressed out.

My favourite is seeing people walk towards a shop, nearly get there and then go "Oh sh*t" and run back to their car for their mask. Mum literally has masks EVERYWHERE, jean's pockets, jacket pockets, handbags and loads all over the car. It's a bit like all the pairs of glasses all over the house - she can never find them - usually they are on her head.

Neville said she's slowly turning into Grandma. He said she'll be doing Sudoku and watching the Midsomer Murders next.

13th August

The A' level results came out today. According to Grandpa it's "an absolute fiasco." Em's older sister is completely devastated. Her grades are totally not what she needs. She wants to study Economics (no idea why - sounds REALLY boring) and so didn't get her University place that she wanted even though she's always got really high marks for everything. They are way below what she was predicted to get.

Neville said that because the exams got cancelled, the Government used an algorithm, which was a total disaster. Loads of people are really angry and upset about it.

Seems to me that there isn't much they are getting right at the moment. People are angry with them a lot of the time.

16th August

There's been protests in cities all across the UK about the results. A bunch of students were outside the department of Education holding big placards and shouting "f**k the algorithm."

19th August

Me and Tom played mini-golf today with Em and Jack. They are going out now which is BRILLIANT, because we can do stuff together. It's good not being the only one in our group with a boyfriend.

Em's sister is all sorted - the Government admitted the algorithm had been really unfair on lots of kids and they changed their mind. Em's grades were changed and now she's going to this University in

London that is the top one for people doing Economics, which was what she wanted. I told Auntie Ellie because she's the only person in the family that would be even remotely interested. She said it was "absolutely marvellous."

20th August

GCSEs came out today. OMG - that will be ME next year. IF we do the GCSEs at all that is…

After the algorithm thing with the A' levels, the teachers assessed the grades so it was all a lot fairer. Most of the people I know in year 11 are happy, and got what they needed so that's good. Still really jealous they didn't have to actually sit the exams though.

It's still really HOT and sunny, but I am SO over sunbathing. Everyone in town is really fed up because the park is absolutely PACKED every single day. There are cars everywhere. People are coming from all over the place to have picnics and swim in the lake. There is so much RUBBISH everywhere it's totally DISGUSTING. Why don't people just take it home with them. Mum says it's why the planet is in such a mess - human beings not caring. She's sad because she thought the virus would make people care more and behave differently, but everything is just the same.

Neville says people are even "crapping in the bushes," because all the public toilets are locked because of Covid. OMG. REVOLTING!

Mum says it will be people having days out because they can't go abroad on holiday (or don't want to) so they are all here, and they shouldn't be here. It's crazy, it's a free country. You can't stop people visiting places .. in fact her and Neville have been talking about going to Oxford for the day. She said that was different when I pointed it out.

Neville just muttered, "staggering hypocrisy." He likes that phrase.

24th August

Tom came over, we all went to hang out at the park - even though it's so busy.

Mum had suggested we stay at home - she said we could all sunbathe in the garden and Neville could put the BBQ on later.

Yeah right !! We'd have to deal with the two of them being TOTALLY embarrassing. Like I'd agree to that.

I lied and said it had been arranged for ages and we were all getting pizza in town with an Eat Out to Help Out voucher. She said, "Well that sounds like lots of fun," and put on a big smile, but I could tell she was disappointed. I felt a bit bad actually.

We saw Izzy in town, I pretended that I hadn't seen her even though she was waving frantically. I just grabbed Tom's hand and crossed the street. That's my BOYFRIEND's hand Izzy. I've got a really great boyfriend that you can't STEAL this time!

Literally the BEST thing about lockdown, and so many people rushing off on holidays abroad, is that I haven't had to put up with her and the Ms and all of their TOTAL DRAMA for months and months.

30th August

So it's the Bank Holiday weekend, which is normally a nice long weekend in the sun and a day off work tomorrow.

Well I'm sick of spending all day in the sun, and I'm sick of days off. I'd quite like a day back at work actually. The papers are all talking about how it's safe for all the kids to go back to school and it's safe for everyone to get back to the office. In fact they're saying you SHOULD get back to the office because you'll probably keep your job if you don't. People working at home are more "vulnerable to job losses."

Talking of the papers - get this. A few days back I took the dog for a walk and we had a nice pint of Ale and a bag of crisps outside the pub, in the sunshine. Well I had the Ale and she had most of the crisps, after she jumped up and knocked the packet all over the ground. It was incredibly nice to sit there with a pint and feel a bit of normality. Anyway someone had left a copy of The Daily Star of all things lying on another table, so I grabbed it for a read.

Front cover .. in all seriousness - photo of one of those big lumps of kebab meat. Headline reads "Gonna Kebab" and, I kid you not, it was an article predicting "Bank Holiday chaos" as the UK stands to RUN OUT of kebab meat over the Bank Holiday weekend due to the huge numbers of people that are 'staycationing' in the UK.

Seriously .. this is what we've come to as a Nation? Eating so much kebab meat that we face an actual SHORTAGE of the stuff. No wonder the Government was blaming the number of Covid cases on obesity!

And "staycation" .. don't get me on that one. Staying in your own HOME and going to local places of interest is a STAYCATION. Going on holiday in the UK is a HOLIDAY!!!

So if you are one of those people that has cleaned out your local kebab house this weekend, or you use the term staycation .. you can DO ONE.

4th September

I went back to school today - so stupid starting on a Friday. The new little year 7's started yesterday so they could get used to it without everyone there. It's weird. We are all in bubbles in different bits of the school. We have to wear masks in the corridors and the canteen is shut. Everyone has to use the sanitisers all over the school and the stuff is really hard to get out of them so most people just use their own.

7th September

School is a nightmare - we have tons and tons of tests to work out how behind we all are from not being at school. Some people worked really hard at home and some people did absolutely nothing. I don't see why I have to do more work because some people couldn't be bothered. Mum says it's not that at all, it's so the teachers can assess how to get everyone sort of back to the same place.

The rules in school are really stupid - everyone's careful all day, all the year groups are separated in different bits of the school We social distance in the corridors and do everything properly and we wear our masks, but once we are outside it doesn't count so when the bell goes everyone just piles out at the same time. Then everyone just barges into each other and stands round chatting in groups, and no one has their masks on anymore … and then some people even hug each other goodbye.

Honestly. Waste of time. And we have another stupid Boris 3 part slogan thing to follow..

"Hands - Face - Space"

I know they pay some idiot a fortune to make these stupid things up, but what's the point if half the people in the Country are ignoring it ….

Neville keeps saying … "what's this new one again .. "Hands - Arse - Spoon" was that it?"

8th September

Today there was an earthquake ….. In Leighton Buzzard !!

I am SO shocked … but Neville just shrugged and said it's "bang on for 2020" and "the Zombie's can't be too far off now."

9th September

Mum's been on WhatsApp for hours, they are planning their big weekend away, a couple of people can't go anymore, but they seem to have loads to discuss .. sounds like it's all to do with food and taxis and how much alcohol to pack !

Helen's not happy because she's had to go back to school and be a dinner lady again. She was really enjoying furlough. She said that the virus is really handy though, because when the horrible little kids that she doesn't like try to hold her hand or sit on her knee, she can just shout "COVID" and say "sorry, you're not allowed to come near me."

10th September

Mum keeps totally BUGGING me about when they can meet Tom "properly." She still has a total thing about me talking to HIS parents and him not talking to her and Neville. I had to promise it would be soon. I might invite him when she's away with the gang. That way it's only Neville. He's an idiot, but in fairness he doesn't float about in ridiculous clothes going on about auras.

19th September

Mum's gone off on her girls weekend. Luckily a couple of them couldn't go, otherwise there would have been more than 6 and that would have been really awkward, because Boris just introduced this Rule of 6 thing a few days ago. It would have messed up where they were staying and going out for lunch and everything.

I didn't invite Tom whilst she's away. It felt a bit too mean.

22nd September

So Boris was on TV again tonight - Neville spent all day yesterday going on about how they'd be announcing a second lockdown. Turned out it was just telling the pubs to shut a bit earlier. You'd have thought from the fuss that Neville made that we'd just been told we were back in Lockdown for a whole year.

It's ONE HOUR !

He was furious !! The pubs now have to shut at 10pm instead of 11pm .. I really can't see what difference that will make. There are tons of jokes now about the fact the virus will only kill you after 10pm and you are fine up until then.

It's not funny though - most people aren't really taking it seriously any more but Mum knows 3 people now that have died from Coronavirus and they weren't all old people either. Another guy she worked with years ago had it in April and he's still really ill, he can't walk very far without getting out of breath and he sleeps for hours every day. He hasn't gone back to work full time because it's too hard for him. I try not to read too much about it as it's a bit scary. It felt worse before though because everyone was scared .. now people don't really seem to care. Even lots of the old people are out without masks on and standing close to each other chatting.

Neville insisted on going straight to the pub after Boris had finished talking to "just to enjoy that extra hour for the last time." He really is an idiot.

24th September

So the curfew in the pub doesn't seem to be making much difference. Neville showed me a news video from London where people all got kicked out of the pubs at 10 o'clock so they were buying beer in the Tesco's express shops and standing in the street drinking and chatting to people. Everywhere was really busy. So much for making things safer. I said I thought it was crazy and Neville said, "well the virus was waiting patiently for them to come out of the pub so it doesn't have to go in there and find them. Everything's fine up until 10.00pm."

He thinks he is so funny.

People are still dying though so it's not actually funny at all.

26th September

I invited Tom over because Mum and Neville have gone ON AND ON about wanting to meet him. I've been totally dreading it and avoided it as long as possible by going over to his house. I told them that they weren't allowed to be totally weird and annoying like they normally are. They said they would try.

Mum was working on her laptop in the lounge when he arrived so she just said, "Hello". I thought she'd start being weird, but that was it - mind you, she did say it in a sort of squeaky high voice - like on Kevin and Perry! Neville was making a coffee in the kitchen and said, "alright mate how's it going?"

We hung out in my room all afternoon, because it was pouring with rain and then he went home. They both said "bye" to him, but NOTHING else - luckily !! After he'd gone they were really keen to find out if they'd been OK or if they'd embarrassed me. I said it was fine and they hadn't been too bad. Neville said, "great, so we weren't too bad, mainly because we barely spoke to him or looked at him the whole time he was here." I said "yeah basically."

27th September

Neville here .. blimey it's all going on to be honest with you .... Top rants today are :

Pub Curfew : Waste of time .. it's not making any difference - all that is happening is that the people that want to get hammered just go in the pub a bit earlier and order double rounds so they don't miss out. If anything they are drinking more and drinking quicker .. which leads to them to totally forget social distancing and start hugging their mates. And they forget to put the masks on to go to the toilets, don't check in on the Tracing App (not that it works anyway) and then everyone piles out at exactly the same time all close together. Pointless. Totally f'ing pointless. Oh ..... And guess which bar DOESN'T have a 10pm curfew? Yep ... the bar in the House of Commons. This lot really do take us for a bunch of muppets.

Anti-Maskers : Right .. that lot. Seriously don't get me started on them. Mass gathering of the Covidiot anti-mask brigade yesterday. They were out in force in Trafalgar Square. No masks obviously, complaining about their civil liberties and listening to speeches by David Icke. David bleedin' Icke of all people. Now here's a man that claims the world is run by reptiles and that the Royal Family are ACTUALLY lizards. I mean some of them aren't particularly attractive, I'll give you that, but that's where in-breeding gets you. But lizards? And people actually follow this nutter? I'd say I was surprised, but seriously nothing ever surprises me anymore.

Rules about Groups: There's now a £10,000 fine for people who are breaking the law and meeting in big groups. The Government is telling people to report their neighbours if they are breaking the law - like if there are too many people in the house or if they are supposed to be in quarantine and they go out. We wouldn't last 2 minutes trying to break the law, because Derek and Doreen are on 24 hour surveillance duty watching EVERY SINGLE PERSON in the road! I'm pretty sure I've spotted binoculars at the window. The second the rule of six is broken they'll be straight on the phone to the Rozzers.

Weddings are down to 15 people now from 30 - my mate at work managed to change his numbers from about 120 .. just about get away with 30 without really upsetting anyone and now it's 15 ... absolute joke! 30 people allowed at a funeral though ... so how's that different? Aside from one of them being dead? He even asked whether they would be allowed 30 guests if the ushers carried the bride into the Church in a coffin. Apparently the answer is no. Also, he offended the vicar.

But get this .. you can have 30 people to go grouse shooting - 'cos that's something vitally important to loads of the population isn't it? Talk about keeping the posh gits happy. I told him to hire a country estate, get some grouse and a few guns and if one of the grouse-shooters just happens to be in a big fancy white dress then so be it. Or Polo .. you could have 30 people if you fancy getting married playing polo.

Also this month scientists said they'd found life on Venus .. maybe we are due an Alien Invasion to top the year off. The zombies never came after all. To be honest I'd swop the current Government for aliens in a heartbeat.

I dunno ... Jack even called this afternoon saying he couldn't get to his hospital appointment on time because of a massive sinkhole in the road. Course there was a sinkhole ... that's totally on-brand for 2020.

*So that's it ... f***ing grouse-shooting toffs can do ONE and so can the David Icke followers.*

28th September

Ella has gone back to University - she's only been there a few days and her student halls have got locked down. She's not allowed to leave. Auntie Sally drove to Liverpool with a massive food parcel for her. She had to meet her by the gate and hand it over, she couldn't even go in. Loads of students have tested positive so they are stuck in their halls self-isolating. Uncle Dave is furious - it's costing him £9,000 for Ella to be stuck in a building doing her studying online. He said she might as well have done it from home, but she said the pubs are better in Liverpool.

The students have put signs in the windows saying stuff like "HM Prison," "F**k you Boris" and "Tory B**tards. They've been told they have to take them down or they will be thrown out .. that's a joke since they can't actually leave. The sign on Ella's window just says, "Help … send beer !"

Mum said it's stupid complaining about protest signs - she said students have always protested and put signs in windows. She said when she was at university everyone was protesting against nuclear war. Their posters were all signs with a symbol on for the CND - which was the campaign for nuclear disarmament. She said there was a big hand-stitched banner on the front of their halls of residence with the CND sign on and the words "people that can't sew very well against the bomb."

Grandpa even got arrested taking part in a CND protest when he was younger. He's quite proud of that. Mum says that fighting for nuclear disarmament was the same as fighting for climate change for previous generations.

29th September

Right Neville here :

So the Covid numbers are going up again and APPARENTLY it's all our fault .. yes that's US. The public.

It's got nothing to do with the Government encouraging people to rush off on holiday abroad in July, and telling them to get down the pub again and launching Eat Out to Help Out through the whole of August.

It's got nothing to do with the idiots in charge of Track and Trace being incapable of doing the job. So the testing system isn't working, despite the fact that the Government spaffed 12 billion to get the job done. Maybe if they picked people that knew what they were doing that might have helped.

It's got nothing to do with all the confusing messages. So Boris makes statements like "the rules are simple," then when he's asked about one of them on a trip up North, manages to get it completely wrong. He made the rules up. If he doesn't understand them, there's not much hope for anyone else.

So here's a little monthly summary of how things are going so far now ....

Feb: Be Kind
March: Get in a fist fight in ASDA over the last 4-pack of bog roll
April: Do the shopping for a pensioner and become a caring member of your local community.
May : Get angry with pensioners for not following the rules
June: Get angry with ALL the Covidiots for not following the rules
July: Get hammered at the pub - it's your patriotic duty
August: Eat out at the pub - it's your patriotic duty
Sept : You've only got yourselves to blame for not following the rules and for being too obese to fight the virus successfully. Oh and please report your mates if they break the rules.

1st October

Wow it's October already … seems like the year has gone really fast AND really slow at the same time - especially since we haven't actually done anything.

Well I say that - I've done loads ! I've had all my school work and loads of stress!

Mum has sort of worked a bit, but mostly spent time putting on weight. All her friends go on about the "Covid Stone" or they say 19 pounds is what the number stands for in COVID-19. I'm surprised it's not more to be honest, with the amount of drinking they all did and are STILL doing.

Neville went back to work a couple of weeks ago. Well not BACK, he's still here, working at home. He had a pretty nice holiday I think, but is still moaning about having to work again. He is back doing EXTREMELY loud conference calls with a shirt on top and pjs on the bottom and using the term "Zoom compliant" to describe his outfit. Annoying.

He's also back shouting annoying things with his headphones in. At least I'm at school now and don't have to deal with him during the day. I know it's really annoying Mum though, she was hoping they'd want him to be back in the actual office.

All because he's been working from the spare room again, he sold the treadmill she bought at the beginning of lockdown. That annoyed her, even though she literally used it 3 times since March.

2nd October

So TRUMP has got the Coronavirus now .. him and his wife (who still looks miserable the WHOLE time) both tested positive.

Neville said, “I wonder if, right now, there’s some poor sod from The White House syphoning disinfectant up Trump’s arse?”

Mum said, “Stop it Neville - I don’t want to think about that. Now, I dislike negative vibes and I don’t like to wish anyone ill - especially not with this horrible disease - but maybe he will have to step down with ill health? That would be a great result.”

5th October

Trump has only been in the hospital for 3 days and they’ve already let him out. Neville muttered, “publicity stunt, just like Boris, except they didn’t even bother to pretend he went into the ICU.” The news said he marched into The White House, took his mask off when he should have still been wearing it, and announced, “I’m better and maybe I’m immune.”

12 October

We’ve got a country-wide 3 tier system now. More stuff to be confused about!

It’s supposed to be related to how many cases you have. So towns without many cases can do more normal stuff (like go to the pub) and towns with lots of cases can’t do anything and have to have a sort of local lockdown. It’s mostly places up North that are having to shut down.

13th October

It’s my 16th Birthday today … Seriously 16 !!

I should totally have been in London hanging out in some trendy cafe and plastering the pictures all over instagram or having an amazing party, but instead we are sitting at home wondering if everything is going to go into lockdown again.

At the moment it's still the lowest tier where we live so we can meet 6 people indoors and the pub is still open (literally the ONLY thing that matters to Neville). It means I can still meet my friends, and of course we are STILL having to go to school.

We did a family Zoom and Ella joined from Liverpool to say Happy Birthday.

Hiya Ruby - Happy 16th mate ! Everything's well exciting up here Ruby. Actual Robert Pattinson's here being Batman!! It's amazing that THIS is somewhere the famouses want to come. Dunno why they would. But anyway, some kids were shouting "Goth Nonce" at him across the street. Proper funny ! But I might have to come back home soon, cos the 'Rona's kicking off a bit here - loads of new infections and that - we're going into Tier 3 or something soon .. means I can still go to 'Spoons 'cos they serve food yeah, but only with my flatmates - cos they are like my bubble? And we have to sit and eat a proper meal to get any drinks. All the other places are gonna shut. We can drink in the flat, but it's not that much fun if I can't see anyone else .. so I might come home."

I'm SO jealous about her seeing Robert Pattinson!! But it sounds like it wasn't up very close.

So I didn't see an actual Hollywood star on my birthday, but I did get some great presents. Mum and Neville got me a TV for my room which is cool - even though Mum has "a thing" about TVs in bedrooms. I got loads of clothes and stuff to decorate my room - lights, photo frames and stuff like that.

Mum got me a really lovely cake with my name on a rose gold cake topper thing saying Happy Sweet 16 Ruby. Grandpa said that "sweet sixteen" is another stupid American thing that's made it's way over here, but Grandma told him to shut up and not "not spoil Ruby's birthday."

Since we are spending ALL day together at school, my friends came for a sleepover - only 4 of them though so we could still do the

#Ruleof6 thing and not get into trouble or get fined or anything. We wouldn't normally do a school night, but no one seems to care anymore.

Mum just said, "to hell with it, if we go back into lockdown at least you had a nice day."

18th October

We went away for the weekend. It was exciting. I've only been to see family for the last 6 months. It was kind of nice staying somewhere different. Mum decided to drag us to Glastonbury, which was actually quite cool. We had an Airbnb with a lovely view and it was sunny all weekend so there were pretty sunsets.

When we went into town Neville decided we should play "Glastonbury Bingo" and listed a bunch of stuff to tick off a list.

Stuff like:

A druid
Someone with a very long wizard beard
4 pairs of flared trousers
Someone playing the bongos
Someone playing the recorder
Someone smoking weed in plain sight
Someone with very long dreadlocks

We saw all of them in about 10 minutes flat, so it wasn't a very hard game. I asked if I could have a bonus because the bongo player (that I happened to spot) had flared trousers, very long dreadlocks and was also smoking weed in plain sight. Mind you so was everyone else to be honest. The whole town smelt of weed. The druid appeared to be wearing a crocheted dress, but that wasn't on our list.

We went into some really cool shops selling witchcraft stuff and Mum got like a MILLION new crystals.

We went to this really peaceful meditation garden thing with special spring water. Mum and Neville also walked up this big hill thing that is supposed to be famous, but I didn't bother with that, it sounded like it might be hard work.

On the way home we apparently drove past Stonehenge, but I was asleep and I missed it.

24th October

We went to see Auntie Sophie and Uncle Marc's new house. They moved out of London just after the lockdown eased up and now they have a lovely garden and are nearer to Grandma and Uncle Dave, which is really nice. They go to a little village school linked to the Church. Last week Coco came home, stood in the kitchen with her arms outstretched, and announced "Jesus is Light" to everyone.

Coco was sad to leave her old school and especially Horatio and Badger, but she's made new friends called Indigo and Octavia and now she loves her new school. Neville thinks Felix's friends all sound like old blokes from the East End. They are called Alfie, Bertie and Ted.

Coco has started violin lessons and so she was showing me her violin. Auntie Sophie got Felix a little Ukulele so he didn't feel left out. Coco's only had about 2 lessons, but she can STILL read music better than I could after about 4 months! I told her I used to play the violin and decided to see what I remembered. I had a go with the bow and played a tune. I was quite pleased given it was a long time since I'd played, but she told me I was doing it wrong even though she's only plucking the strings and hasn't even learnt how to use the bow yet.

She also asked me why I had such a spotty face. I've got like 4 small pimples on my forehead !

Kids are VERY DIRECT. We went for a lovely walk in the woods earlier in the afternoon and she made me climb a tree with her. Then she told me I wasn't very nimble! RUDE.

We all had a lovely dinner and then Coco and Felix went to bed. I went to watch Strictly on my own in the lounge because the so-called adults were drinking loads and yelling song titles at Alexa. Mum and Auntie Sophie went to bed when the boys decided that Jaegerbombs were a good idea. Uncle Marc was still on the sofa in the morning and Neville was in a very bad mood because Felix woke him up at 5am, when he came running into the bedroom playing his Ukulele.

26th October

The more things that happen each day, the more stuff Neville is loading onto YouTube. For that reason alone I wish things would get sorted and we could go back to normal. He said 2020 is just writing his material for him.

Here's his latest rant on the free school meals situation:

*Alright people, Neville here - and today is another day of "WTF are they doing now" in the good old UK. Pretty much all the Tory MPs voted AGAINST providing free school meals to kids in the holidays .. the evil b**tards. I mean even Marie bleedin' Antoinette said, "Let them eat cake." They aren't even being that generous .. they are being more .. "nah you can just go without while we eat subsidised fillet steak and drink subsidised Champagne in Westminster. Oh and that Starbucks coffee & pastry I got this morning on the way in? I won't pay for that out of my own pocket, like other people that pick up a snack on their way to work, oh no I will just expense that on top of my massive salary." Seriously - absolute twats. They've made some sh*t decisions during this whole pandemic, but voting to let kids starve?? This won't be forgotten quickly - you mark my words.*

Mind you a couple of months ago they were telling us we are all OBESE, which is rich coming from a fine physcial specimen like

Boris, so maybe starving the kids is their way to fight the obesity epidemic we are supposedly facing??

*They can afford to spunk £12 billion to their buddies for the failed test and trace system, and millions on dodgy PPE contracts to companies that don't know how to make PPE, and a bridge that never got built and a ferry contract to a company without any ferries, and the train that gets you to Birmingham 20 minutes quicker ... the list goes on ..... oh yeah .. AND they can award themselves a nice little pay rise. The NURSES don't deserve one apparently, but that shower of sh*t do. For WHAT ?? .. for f***ing up the whole country ?? ..... So yeah .. plenty of dosh for all that, but little bit more so some kids don't go hungry .. nah, no magic money tree for that apparently.*

Twitter is seriously kicking off, and local councils are now deciding they are going to sort it themselves.

*And you know the real irony of this, don't you?? If each of those vulnerable kids was a consultant they'd find them £7000 a day no bother .. but right now they can't find them £7 a day. Perhaps all the kids need to retrain like in that sh*tty ballerina advert. Fatima was happy dancing you clueless twats, she doesn't want to work in Cyber.*

Some twat of an MP up North said that giving free school meals over the summer holiday was effectively "giving money to brothels and crack dens." So he isn't keen to do it again. He's an MP - doesn't he know they give out vouchers for this? Vouchers for FOOD only ... they aren't handing out hard cash to kids on the corner of every housing estate. I'd like to see someone trying to buy drugs with a dodgy ham sandwich and a cereal bar.

So local businesses are doing their bit and stepping up to help feed some of the kids in need. Then what happens ... this woman MP ACTUALLY has a go at these businesses FOR TRYING TO HELP - saying they must be doing alright if they can afford to give stuff away and so they shouldn't need any more Covid-19 support from the Government. Nice. They are doing what you should be doing, you odious human being.

*Oh and let's not forget the Tory Councillor that suggested people should "sell their pearls" if they can't afford to feed their kids. "Cos we all just have valuable pearls lying about the place. YOU COULD NOT MAKE THIS SH*T UP.*

*Meanwhile .. it's nearly November so it will be Covid's 1st birthday before too long ... can you believe that ??? ... China kept its birth a bit quiet, but I reckon people will make a bit of a fuss now it's gonna be a whole year old! What shall we all do to celebrate? We can't have a rave as it's illegal, or a get together with more than 2 households, or more than 6 people. You can't invite an old person or hug anyone and you certainly can't go to a f***ing panto. And if you live up North you can't even go to the pub .. well you probably can as long it's somewhere you can eat a pie - but you have to have chips with the pie or it's not considered a "substantial meal." Only substantial meals are keeping the pubs open.*

*Perhaps we could use all the "Bat-themed" party crap that we won't be using for Halloween this year and have a jolly get together with the people we are already stuck indoors with. That is we have enough money to buy a sh*tting prawn ring and some hula hoops !*

*Or maybe - in Covid's honour - our nasty corrupt Government could bung a few more BILLION at one of their mates to f**k up something else right up. Worked a treat on the Test, Track and Trace system ...*

So NO ... pretty much the only thing I'll be celebrating is the fact that my Dad is still in one piece, despite what the Tories have done to care homes and that even though I can't visit him, I will be thankful that he's being looked after by ACTUAL living angels !!

So, yeah, NHS workers I salute you, care workers I salute you, Marcus Rashford I salute you. The woman who called the Tories "scum" in Parliament I salute you.

And Boris?

Yep - say it with me - Boris can just DO ONE !!!

28th October

Everyone is pretty down at the moment because things are really miserable again. Seems like we can't go anywhere and they are talking about Christmas being just your own family and no one else. That makes me really sad as we always see Grandma and Grandpa at Christmas. And I STILL haven't been able to hug them since March !!!

It doesn't help that it's rained for the WHOLE of half term. But at least Strictly is back on and the Bake Off AND Taskmaster. Although a bunch of boomers have been complaining because there's a same sex couple on Strictly and some people think it's disgusting. I don't know what is wrong with people - they are SOOO old fashioned. Half my generation are LGBT.

I have loads of studying to do. I wish they'd just say the GCSEs are cancelled.

I haven't seen Tom AT ALL over half-term - he's had to self-isolate because more kids at his school have had symptoms. Mum keeps bugging me about when they can meet him again and actually talk to him properly. It's actually a bit of a relief that he literally CAN'T visit us right now. I can just delay the embarrassment.

Auntie Sally went up to Liverpool to bring Ella home from University since things are getting worse up in the North. Neville keeps muttering "Tell them The North remembers" in an ominous voice. [Something to do with Game of Thrones .. he's a bit obsessed with that programme].

Mum has got a part-time job delivering testing kits for some market research company her friend told her about, so she's earning a bit of money from that and doing a few hours at the cafe when she's needed.

And Ollie - SERIOUSLY - Ollie has actually become a YouTube SENSATION !!

He doesn't even have time for the cafe anymore - he's put managers in charge of opening the other two shops and spends all his time on promotions and sponsorship deals. Neville gets annoyed every time he pops up on his feed with videos and ads saying stuff like, "If I could pivot successfully during a global pandemic, you can too," and "you can smash it online and earn 6 figures just like me. Follow my 3 step success formula NOW."

Oh and I forgot .. THE BIGGEST NEWS of all. YES … after just 6 months of constant effort and a lot of anger Neville finally baked a loaf of Sourdough bread!! It was really nice actually and he is SO proud of himself.

He said, "I never gave up Ruby, I never lost the faith, it's a triumph of the human spirit against the odds."

Bit much. It's just a loaf of bread.

29th October

Neville here again .. with another episode of "Do One Boris."

Seriously - there's so much shit going on - it's a full time job keeping up.

The infection numbers are going up again and people are saying we are pretty much back to the position we were in March. And yet there are STILL a bunch of COVIDIOT Anti-Maskers out there going on about the virus NOT being real and their human rights being attacked.

Twats.

Seriously.

*Someone from the NHS was actually BEATEN UP and thrown OFF a train in London for telling three people that they should have masks on when using public transport. F***king beaten up !!!!*

The world's gone MENTAL.

This stupid 3 Tier system is buggered - cases are still rising and other countries are going back into full lockdowns. Not us though .. OH NO. We are just jollying along, keeping the pubs open .. in some places you can only keep the pub open if you serve food - so a pint and food is a better defence against Covid than just a pint on it's own. Wales is shut again and you can only buy essential things - so you can get beer in Tescos, but you can't get a birthday card in the post office or a pair of socks in a clothes shop. SO that's kicking off - people are complaining that if a clothes shop or card shop on the high street has to shut then people shouldn't be able to get their socks and cards in Tescos instead. Quite right. The massive supermarkets are the people that have carried on raking it in all through the pandemic anyway!! So people are covering up the shelves in certain sections of shops.

Not a problem in England though where all the odious humans that call themselves The Cabinet are happy for all the shops to be open and for everyone to just DIE!

Speaking of odious humans, that witch Priti Patel is pretending to be sorry about some migrants who just drowned attempting to cross the channel - including two little kids. She said she was "truly saddened to learn of the tragic loss of life". DO ME A FAVOUR - this is the woman that wanted to put a wave machine in the channel to stop people trying to come over here in boats! And before that, she wanted to send asylum seekers to camps on a volcanic island in the middle of nowhere. Putting people you don't like into camps ... hmmmmmm .. when did that happen before ...

*And I'll tell you something for nothing ... things would have to be SERIOUSLY sh*t in another Country for anyone to decide the UK is a better bet right now !*

Oh and I forgot ... Boris has also said that the Police will have the power to enter people's homes and break up their Christmas dinners if they go against any of the new rules. I wonder if that will apply to Dominic Cummings and his mates from Specsavers? Or Boris Johnson's Dad, who will probably fly a bunch of his friends over from Greece for a big knees up ...... it won't really matter if they are all grouse shooting ... or playing Polo.

So we are on for a "World Beating" Christmas by the sounds of it.

So see you another day, but for now ...

Priti Patel can DO ONE, Boris can DO ONE and apparently Christmas can DO ONE now as well.

31th October

It's Halloween - the little kids aren't supposed to be trick or treating, public firework displays are cancelled next week and now Boris is coming on TV later, which everyone says means there will be another Lockdown.

Neville said if they're doing another lockdown why don't they JUST get on with it … Instead they will probably wait a few more days - just so people get to have a bit more time in the pub before all the toilet roll buying and competitive breadmaking starts again. That's rich coming from him .. he's completely and utterly OBSESSED with his Sourdough starter now he's produced an actual loaf.

This also means he's back on furlough again. He literally JUST went back to actual work.

Mum said he shouldn't have been so quick to sell her treadmill. She's all enthusiastic again, and DETERMINED to do Lockdown2 differently to the first time. She's talking about cooking nutritional winter food, losing weight, not drinking very much and doing 30 days of Yoga with Adrienne this time.

And Me? Well I don't feel THAT different to be honest - I'm just outside less and in my room more - especially now it's getting colder.

3 November

Everyone is pretty miserable again apart from Martha. She's thoroughly looking forward to Lockdown2, because she gets to do it without being locked in the house with Terence.

Mum is miserable, her good mood didn't last long. She was really enjoying going to see her friends again and visiting family, having the odd weekend away, and going out to dinner at people's houses. She said she can't face going back to doing everything on Zoom again. She keeps saying Lockdown1 was so much easier because it was sunny and it was a bit of a novelty. Now we know what to expect, it's just depressing. But she did say she's going to dig out her "hobby" list and try to do all the stuff she didn't do the first time round. I'll believe that when I see it!

Neville is miserable, because he'll have to go back to drinking in his shed instead of down the pub, but he said it's pros and cons .. because if he's on furlough again he can just play on his Xbox. Mum disagreed and said if he's on furlough again he can paint the kitchen and sort out the vegetable patch.

I'm miserable because they are literally closing EVERYTHING, but I still have to go to school. All the infections are going up since we went back to school and the older ones went back to University. Even I can see that's a problem .. and I'm RUBBISH at Science … Why can't the Government see that?

I really want them to close the schools. If that happens we won't be able to do the mocks and if we can't do mocks we might not be able to do actual exams. That would be THE BEST.

I liked doing online lessons anyway and so many people are having to isolate waiting for test results, that the teachers are already live streaming pretty much every lesson anyway.

It's definitely closer to home this time. Lots of people know people that are getting tested now and some of Mum's friends have had positive results back, we are just hoping they have a mild reaction and don't get the really bad version.

The other big news is everybody waiting to see if Trump will get voted in again as President … I really hope not .. seems to me he's completely insane. It's also a bit mad that the ONLY people they can find to be possible Presidents are both in their 70s. They should be retired and having a nice time playing games like golf and bowls followed by a pint, and a bit of lunch, just like Grandpa does.

6th November

It's the 6th of November now and the election in America seems to have been going on for a MILLION days. It looks like Trump is going to lose, but he's not taking it well and accusing everyone else of cheating and is generally carrying on like a kid having a massive tantrum. I wish they'd just announce it either way so Mum and Neville stop going on about it. According to Neville even if Trump does lose, he won't be out of The White House until January so anything could happen in a couple of months.

Ellie put in the family WhatsApp that she thought it was really marvellous that Greta Thunberg trolled him back for his anger management comments last year and told him he needed to chill.

Boris was on TV again telling us Lockdown2 will only last for 4 weeks, and it will all be over by Christmas. Mum says that's what another politician famously said before and it didn't turn out too well. Weird coincidence his name was Neville!

Our Neville played "Boris Bingo" with Mum during the press conference - this is where they tick off any typical words that Boris might use … here's a few examples;

Resilient
Ramping up
Unprecedented
Tremendous

Marvellous
World-Beating
New Normal
Success/Successful/Succeeding
Confident
All in this together
NHS Track and Trace (big emphasis on the word NHS)

Neville says it's not run by the NHS, it's run by someone called Serco and is another example of Boris "spaffing money up the wall." He says they just keep saying NHS, so they can blame them later on for it being a failure.

I don't really mind about Lockdown2. It was alright last time. And I've got Strictly, Taskmaster and Googlebox to keep me happy. Mum says the new season of The Crown is coming soon as well.

Neville said, "I can't wait for "The Crown .. The Spaffer Years." That'll be worth a watch …

7th November

A bunch of people in my year are self-isolating because Dan, Jake, Connor and both the James' have ALL been in contact with covid positive people.

They finally announced that Joe Biden is going to be the next president and Trump is done. Neville said they will most likely need the secret service to drag him out of The White House kicking and screaming like a two year old being removed from the toy aisle in ASDA.

So I said, "or YOU after last orders in the old days when the pub was a thing."

He thought that was quite funny.

Jaime said people are actually dancing in the streets in America they are so happy. Uncle John is a bit quiet on the family WhatsApp.

8th November

The dog is COMPLETELY deranged at the moment because there are endless fireworks.

I couldn't have my hair appointment this week because the hairdressers are shut again - but there's a ton of traffic, everywhere is really, really busy, I still have to go to school and it doesn't feel "lockdowny" at all.

10th November

The GCSEs are now cancelled in Wales - so that's Scotland and Wales .. it's completely unfair that we still have to do ours. I guess there's still a chance that we won't.

THE WHOLE OF YEAR 11 has to self-isolate now, because of all the people testing positive - we keep getting supply teachers filling in on lessons who don't even know what we are doing. It's a joke - they might as well just shut the schools.

Boris promised everything would be sorted in time for Christmas. Any promise from Boris seems pretty unlikely to come true really so I'm not holding my breath .. but I am still really, really sad that this could be the FIRST Christmas in my WHOLE LIFE that I don't spend with Grandma and Grandpa.

And worst of all, I finally have a proper boyfriend, who is COMPLETELY BRILLIANT, and I can't even go and see him. 2020 really has been very very crap!

But Trump is out - so that's some good news. And they've said today that there's a vaccine showing really good results, so things could be looking up and we are ALL really, really hoping that 2021 will be better for everyone.

Here's what Neville had to say to sum it all up …

*Well folks … here we are hurtling towards the season finale of 2020 … I don't know who's been writing this, stuff but seriously …. It's been an absolute sh*tshow of a year. What on earth can they come up with in the next few weeks that will top what we've already been through??*

The Trump thing was a bit of a plot twist, I've gotta be honest, him staying for 4 more years seemed like the most 2020 thing that could happen, but they didn't go for the obvious storyline which is great !

And there's positive talk of a vaccine. All the Covidiot "Wake Up" conspiracy theory people are SERIOUSLY off on one today, ranting away, calling everyone sheep. To be completely honest, at this point I couldn't care less WHAT Bill Gates decided to shove into me .. whatever it is, i'm pretty sure it wouldn't give me as much grief as Windows Vista did for starters. They could stick a 5G mast in the middle of my garden pub and I would lick the damn thing if it meant life went back to normal.

So things are potentially looking up, but trust me the Covidiots are EVERYWHERE. It's been November 5th EVERY single night this week with fireworks going off for hours on end.

Hilariously, theYanks think we are celebrating Biden winning, little do they know we are STILL celebrating the death of someone that committed treason 400 years AGO!! Never say us Brits don't hold a bit of a grudge and hang onto our so-called glorious past.

Some absolute muppets already have Christmas trees up at the beginning of November. And I'm hoping all the parents are so exhausted with homeschooling in lockdown, that they aren't even remotely tempted to get that damn Elf out of it's box!

Meanwhile on Twitter some moron is claiming that the Government has engulfed a load of Northern towns in a strange fog - only the towns that were standing up to the Government mind you - and that they are using the fog as a form of control. Yeah so the Government is forcing people in the North to stay indoors. Through the clever use of fog. In November. Listen, I'm from Manchester, and I can tell you now freezing ice and blizzards wouldn't stop Northern lasses going out if they wanted to, and not only that, they'd do it a mini-skirt and a crop top. So a little bit of fog's not going to swing it.

So yeah .. the latest episode of this dystopian nightmare includes the use of entirely normal autumn weather patterns to control the Northern masses.

So good stuff aside, there's still plenty of weird shit that could happen in the season finale ... I've gotta tell you, my money is on the Zombies finally turning up!

2020 - you can officially DO ONE.

So that's that .. we all need to just wait and see what happens.

To be honest. I'm actually worried the zombies could turn up … Neville's just marched into the garden and put a massive sign on his shed that says "The Winchester."

Acknowledgments

Once again I would like to thank my daughter and husband for their help and support whilst I wrote this.

I would also like to thank them for being great company in Lockdown - we managed to get through without wanting to kill one another.

I would also like to thank friends and family members as ever. For both giving me inspiration and making the whole lockdown easier - even when we couldn't spend time together.

Most of the people in the book are made up - aside from the famous ones!

Those that are based on ordinary "civilians" have kindly given me their blessing to use their stories and personalities.

Table of Contents

1.

2.
3.
4.
5.
6.
7.
8.
9.
10.
11.
12.

4. January 2020
    1.
    2.
    3.
    4.
    5.
    6.
    7.
    8.
    9.
    10.
    11.
    12.
    13.
    14.
    15.
    16.
    17.
    18.
    19.
5. February 2020
    1.
    2.
    3.
    4.
    5.
    6.
    7.

8.
9.
10.
11.
12.
13.
14.
15.

6. March 2020
    1.
    2.
    3.
    4.
    5.
    6.
    7.
    8.
    9.
    10.
    11.
    12.
    13.
    14.
    15.
    16.
    17.
    18.
    19.
    20.
    21.
    22.
7. April 2020
    1.
    2.
    3.
    4.
    5.
    6.
    7.

    8.
    9.
    10.
    11.
    12.
    13.
    14.
    15.
    16.
    17.
    18.
    19.
    20.
    21.
    22.
    23.
    24.
    25.

8. <u>May 2020</u>
    1.
    2.
    3.
    4.
    5.
    6.
    7.
    8.
    9.
    10.
    11.
    12.
    13.
    14.
    15.

9. <u>June 2020</u>
    1.
    2.
    3.
    4.

5.
6.
7.
8.
9.
10.
11.
12.
13.

10. July 2020
    1.
    2.
    3.
    4.
    5.
    6.
    7.
    8.
    9.
    10.
    11.
    12.
    13.
    14.
11. August 2020
    1.
    2.
    3.
    4.
    5.
    6.
    7.
    8.
    9.
    10.
12. September 2020
    1.
    2.
    3.

Printed in Great Britain
by Amazon